Crossed STARS

Crossed STARS

Oak Hills
BOOK 1

PENELOPE FREED

Crossed Stars
Oak Hills Book One

Copyright © 2021 by Penelope Freed

This is a work of fiction. Names, characters, businesses, places, events and incidents are either the products of the author's imagination or used in a fictitious manner. Any resemblance to actual persons, living or dead, or actual events is purely coincidental.

Editing by Corrine Basmaison
Cover and interior design Alt 19 Creative

ISBN: 978-1-7364893-4-5

Romeo

A HAND CLAPS my shoulder a half-second before Marcus bellows above my head. "Ah, parting is such sweet sorrow!" The hallway of crying girls glare at him, a few of them stopping to wave at me with shy smiles, before turning back to comforting each other.

I don't understand why they're all so weepy, it's the end of junior year, we're not graduating or anything. I'll see most of these girls at Rosie's party tonight.

Women.

I love them, but I do not understand them.

"Such a drama queen." I smack Marcus in the stomach with just enough force to prove my point. "Is this your new tactic for getting girls? Quoting Shakespeare?" Benny leans against the lockers beside us, watching as Marcus and I spar in the hallway. Marcus gets in a good hit to my knee before I prance back out of his reach. We play-fight for a little while longer, both of us trusting Benny to let us know if a teacher is heading our way.

"It worked for you didn't it? How else did you score a date with Lexie?" Marcus teases between jabs. "She's out of your league, man."

I grin, letting Marcus get close so I can duck under his arm, pulling it behind his back, and twisting it as I turn to face him.

"Are you sure? Because I think *I* was the one who scored her number, not you. And it was from *The Notebook*, not Shakespeare." Laughing, I move out of Marcus' reach, taking up a position beside Benny, copying his stoic expression. A chorus of high-pitched giggles from the group of girls Marcus and I have been performing for tells me I guessed correctly. What those girls wanted was a little bit of fun so they had a reason to cheer up.

"Ladies." I tip my head in their direction before hooking my arms over Marcus and Benny's shoulders and steering them towards the doors at the end of the hall. The freedom of summer vacation is calling to me. A siren song of sleeping in and girls in bikinis. Does it get any better?

Okay, I can think of one thing better.

Sleeping in and Rosie in a bikini.

"Are you guys coming to Rosie's party tonight?" I ask the group of girls as we pass them. "I'll be devastated if you're not there." I add a wink and a smile, knowing for a fact that Sarah Dempsey still swoons over the dimple in my right cheek, and am rewarded by an air kiss from Tia.

"We'll be there!" Steph calls from the back of the group. "Bye boys."

A couple of girls wave as we pass by, some of them smiling at me, some at my friends. With a face like mine, I've never lacked for girls being interested in me, even though I've never managed to convince one of them to go on more than a few dates.

Something about my over-the-top personality screams "not boyfriend material" on a pheromonal level I guess.

"So, what's this big idea you have planned for tonight?" Marcus blows a kiss to a pack of freshman girls leaning against the wall. I may be the one with a playboy reputation but Marcus is the one who lives up to it. I've never seen him date a girl, but he flirts with all of them equally.

"Have a good summer, Marcus. You too Romeo, Benny," one of the freshman girls is brave enough to respond.

Benny groans and pulls away from me. "Are you seriously still stuck on Rosie? She's never going to be interested in you man. She sees you like a brother. Besides, I know for a fact she told Nikki she's swearing off all dating for the summer. Something about someone coming to stay with her."

We push through the double doors at the end of the hallway and are greeted by the bright glare of afternoon sun, and the heat of an early June day. The Oak Hills Prep parking lot is still pretty full, everyone lingering after the last final to say goodbye or beg a teacher to accept one last assignment. My Jeep Wrangler is already topless, pun intended, and we use the frame to swing inside. Girls dig the way it makes our biceps flex.

"You only say that because you can't get the girl you want." The engine rumbles to life and I pull out of the parking spot. "Besides, my plan is brilliant and you know it."

It has to be brilliant. My penpal and I worked it out years ago and I've been saving it for when I needed to pull out the big guns. And with Rosie, it's go big or go home.

Benny leans into the gap between the two front seats. "And what makes you think you're going to be able to convince everyone who shows up to wear a mask? It's June, not October."

"Because love makes you do crazy things." I give a dramatic sigh, pressing my hand to my chest.

"You're so full of shit, Rome. You don't love Rosie." Marcus drums one hand on the dashboard, his other hand tapping a beat on the frame above his head. The lanky asshole grins, daring me to contradict him. "You've known her since you were kids and it never occurred to you she was attractive until two weeks ago."

"Pfft. That's exactly why I know it must be love this time. I've known her forever. She's not some random chick." I blow a raspberry at my two best friends. "What do you know? You cold-hearted bastards wouldn't know love if it bit you in the nuts." I don't know why I never thought about Rosie in that way before, but something about the way the sunlight touched her blonde hair the other day, when we were driving to school, hit me. She's been a friend for so long, my neighbor, my default friend whenever I was home, it never occurred to me that she could be more.

If the sudden desire I have—to see what she would do if I kissed her—isn't love, what is?

The fact that she's never once looked at me the way other girls do probably had something to do with it. Also the fact that she calls me an over-dramatic pup at least three times a week and a flirtatious bastard every chance she can. But I can change that. I can prove to her that I'm serious this time, that what I feel for her is more than just a passing infatuation.

"Oh, you mean, like how you loved Brittany? Or maybe Barbara? What was her name? The girl from two months ago?" Benny pokes a finger in my ear, reminding me of the string of flings I've had over the years. I can't help it, I love love. And girls. I really love girls.

Marcus and Benny laugh in my face, before Marcus launches into a long speech extolling the virtues of his nuts. I'm too busy driving to follow how he got from talking about defending their virtue to declaring that they probably taste like chocolate and that's why he won't let a girl near them. Benny is rolling with laughter in the backseat and I'm chuckling as I pull up to a party supply store and park.

"Well choco-nut, think you can keep those babies safe long enough to help me out?" I slide out of the Jeep, Benny behind me. "I am in need of supplies."

The boys follow me inside the store and down an aisle exploding with wigs, fake teeth and other costume accessories. "My plan, gentlemen, is to provide masks that the girls will be unable to resist."

"Okay, but seriously, there is no way those masks are going to stop anyone from recognizing each other." Benny points out the flaw in my plan like I haven't already thought of it.

"See, that's what I thought too Benny-boy, until I learned a little secret." I lean close so I can whisper the important tidbit I'd learned from Juliet. "Girls don't want to meet a handsome stranger and be swept off their feet. What they really want, is for the mysterious stranger who sweeps them off their feet to turn out to be the good guy they've known all along. Haven't you ever been forced to watch *You've Got Mail*?" Watching old rom-coms is one of the few things I do with my mom anymore.

I pile a collection of masks, both fancy and plain, in Marcus and Benny's arms before grabbing as many as I can hold, cleaning out the store. Marcus grunts and curses at the masks sliding out of his arms. "Okay, so you buy all the masks in town, then what? You still have to convince everyone to wear them."

I wink at the pretty twenty-something cashier ringing up all the purchases. She rolls her eyes at me but bags them all while I pay. "For starters, the three hottest guys in school are going to be wearing them so that should encourage a lot of people."

Marcus smirks, following Benny and me out the door. "When did you convince Conner and Fitz of this plan? And you haven't convinced me yet."

"Ben, did you hear that?" I fall back against my Jeep, the bags of masks in my hand swinging wide to smack the wheel. "You think Conner and Fitz are hotter than Benny and me? I'm wounded, distraught, inconsolable!"

Marcus groans and Benny smacks me upside the head before taking the bags from me and swinging into the car.

"Ignoring the hurtful words of my former best-friend, I also conveniently happen to live next door. I'll get out there early and get a few of the girls on my side, and before you know it, everyone will be wearing one."

"Get Tia and Steph on board, then all the other girls will do it." Benny has to shout his suggestion over the noise of the wind whipping past the Jeep as we drive home.

"That's brilliant. Can one of you text them? No, wait. I don't trust you assholes. I'll do it myself later."

We rib each other the rest of the drive to Benny's house, where I drop him and Marcus off. "Don't be late, losers!" I call as Benny heads inside and Marcus strolls across the street to his house.

I slump back in my seat as they walk away. This has to work. What girl can resist a masquerade? And my pretty face. Well, lots of girls have resisted my pretty face, but there's no way Rosie will be able to.

Right?

Seventh Grade

DEAR JULIET,

I bet you were expecting a letter from your cousin Rosie, huh? Looks like you're stuck with me instead. Rosie is my next-door neighbor. We've kind of been friends since my family moved in a couple of years ago. We walk to school together most days. I bet you're wondering why I'm the one writing this letter instead of your cousin, right?

We made a bet to see who could sneak into each other's window without getting caught. Let's just say the tree that grows outside my bedroom is much sturdier than the one in her backyard. It's a little hard to be sneaky when you need your dad to take you to the hospital for a broken wrist. But I guess you know all this already. I bet Rosie does too, that's why she made the bet.

The worst part was that I had to miss the playoffs for my baseball team. ~~And now I'm stuck writing these letters to you.~~ Since your mom and Rosie's mom insisted on these letters, the bet was that whoever got caught had to write them. I guess Rosie thinks thirteen is too old for a penpal. Why do you have to write these letters? And why can't you just email like normal people?

Rosie said something about you being homeschooled, but I wasn't really listening. I noticed your address is in Cyprus? I have to be honest with you, I don't even know where that is.

Since I promised Rosie I would write at least one whole page (why is that the minimum? I feel like this is homework), I guess I'll tell you a little about me so you don't feel like you're writing to a complete stranger.

I moved to Oak Hills with my parents five years ago, right after you guys moved away. I live in your old house. Is it weird that I live in your old house? Rosie said your dad works for the government. Is that why you live in another country? What's that like?

My dad is a boring old lawyer and my mom stays home. I just started seventh grade at Oak Hills Middle School. Rosie and I have math together this year. I'm pretty good at math, but my favorite class is P.E. I'm good at lots of sports but baseball is my favorite. I'm planning to try out for the baseball team in high school. I might be able to get my parents to come watch a game if I make varsity one day, which would be cool.

Do they play baseball in Cyprus? Or do they play something else?

Okay, I just looked at a map and now I know where Cyprus is. That's cool that it's almost in Turkey. Do they eat turkey in Turkey? What about Thanksgiving next month? Oh man, I could never give up Thanksgiving. My dad hardly ever has to work on Thanksgiving and it's the only day of the year my mom lets me eat three kinds of pie. Apple, pumpkin, and pecan. All three are my favorites. Do you have a favorite? I can't pick, that's like asking me to pick which is the prettiest girl at school. There are so many pretty girls I have to pick a different one every time Rosie asks me.

Hey, you might have a good answer for this. How do I tell Sarah Dempsey that I think she's cute? Is it weird to leave a note in her backpack at lunch?

Anyways, if you have any good ideas let me know, even if I don't use them on Sarah I'll save them for future reference. Talk to you later!

Later,
ROMEO

DEAR ROMEO,

I'm not sure how I feel about getting a letter from you instead of Rosie. The letters were my mom's idea but I was excited about getting mail. We don't get a lot of mail here at the embassy. We could have just emailed like you said, but there's something special about handwriting a letter, don't you think? It's like something out of an old book.

I read a lot of books out here since there's not many kids on the island and definitely none in the embassy. That's why my mom homeschools me—they don't have an American school here for me to go to and I don't know enough Greek to go to the local school. My mom said it wasn't a good school anyway.

Reading is my favorite thing to do. I just finished re-reading the Harry Potter books. I'm going to read *Anne of Green Gables* next. Do you have a favorite book? Mine has always been *The Chronicles of Narnia*, but it's hard to pick just one.

I would much rather get a real letter than an email, wouldn't you? Although, I guess you'll have to get it from Rosie since I have to mail it to her house, not yours. Are you disappointed you won't get the mail yourself? But I *definitely* can't send mail to a boy. My mom would lose her mind and my dad would have a fit.

I like Cyprus more than Albania, which is where we were last year. The weather is nicer and I can go to the beach here. But I don't go very often. My mom gets nervous when I go outside the embassy without her. So I just stay inside or in the gardens and read my books.

I don't think we have turkeys here, but they usually try to get us one for Thanksgiving. There's a big Thanksgiving dinner here at the embassy but I'm not allowed to have that much pie. How can you eat that much without being sick?

As far as Sarah…I think a note in the backpack is okay. It would be better if you put a flower with it. And signed it "your secret admirer." Every girl wants a letter from a secret admirer.

Let me know how it goes. How's your wrist? Still broken? What are you going to dress up as for Halloween?

Cooped up in Cyprus,
JULIET

CHAPTER THREE

Juliet

I DROP MY bag on the bed and turn to my cousin, exhausted from the long flight and navigating airports on my own. "It's so adorable!" The full-size bed is covered in plain white bedding with gray accents and the walls have black and white photos of Rosie and her brother. But the best part are the dormer windows facing the neighbors house, one of them even has a window seat. My mind fills with visions of curling up in the window like Anne of Green Gables or Catherine Morland with a book I just can't put down.

Thank goodness for ebooks. There is no way my extensive library would have made it through all the moves my family has made in the last few years. Flying here took so long I read my three favorite Jane Austen novels from start to finish—*Pride and Prejudice, Northanger Abbey,* and *Persuasion.*

Rosie looks around. "Eh. It's fine, I guess. Kinda boring."

"I don't care." I pull my suitcase up on the bed beside my bag, unzipping it and pulling clothes out. "Anything is better than the last place we stayed. I wasn't allowed to do anything. I'm so excited to get to have a *normal* summer for once."

Rosie leans against the doorframe, arms crossed as she watches me unpack. "Ugh, this place is so boring. You've lived all over the Mediterranean, I'd kill to have traveled as much as you."

I laugh. She has no idea what my life is like. "When you're the only girl and your parents are as over-protective as mine, you'd be happy to come visit Oak Hills too. I'm just excited to be able to go out on our own, no parents, no escort, no gates or barbed wire fences." I keep pulling clothes out of the bag, refolding them to fit on the empty shelves I spy through the open closet door.

"Are you seriously going to unpack everything right now? Don't you want to relax, hang out? You got here twenty minutes ago, you're allowed to relax."

She has a point. I'm just used to unpacking as quickly as possible since I never know how long I'm going to get to stay in one place. I hate living out of a suitcase, it makes me feel like I don't belong. That's the worst part of having a dad who works for the Foreign Service—we move more often than military families and I'm always starting over. At least I never have to be the new kid at school. Being homeschooled by my mom means that school is never interrupted by something like moving to a different country on a moment's notice.

But that's partly why I'm here. The last embassy we'd been stationed at was a little more unstable than my parents wanted, so they'd packed me up and shipped me off to the States to stay with my aunt and uncle. Since Rosie's older brother Tyson is off at college, they offered for me to come live with them for the summer, maybe even my senior year.

Rosie pushes off the wall, crossing over to hand me a stack of t-shirts. "You know they're not going to send you back for bad behavior, right? You don't have to be Perfect Juliet all the time."

I grin at Rosie's accusation. "I don't know how to be anything else, Rose. My whole life it's felt like I was grounded, but I've never done anything wrong. You can't exactly sneak out of the house when it's guarded by the military." I take the stack Rosie offers, sliding them onto a shelf.

"You may have a point." Rosie concedes. "But now that you're here, I guess we better make it the best summer we can. I'm excited to have someone to hang out with. With Tyson gone, it's so boring." Now that there's a clear space, Rosie falls back on the bed, the arm thrown over her face doing nothing to hide her grin. "I still have two more days of finals and then school is out. Oh!"

I turn from hanging up one of my dresses to see her flipped onto her stomach, feet kicking in the air behind her. "I'm having a 'first day of summer' party on Friday night, so start thinking about what you want to wear."

"What kind of party?" Am I finally going to get to experience a real high school party? And only two days after I get here? This is going to be the best summer ever. "Like, with red solo cups and everything? Will people be..." I swallow hard, glancing to make sure Aunt Cathy and Uncle Chuck aren't nearby. "... drinking?" I finish with a whisper.

Rosie rolls onto her back, laughter exploding from her at my question. "Oh my god, Juliet, you are the most innocent person I know." She doesn't answer my question, just holds her stomach and howls. Her blonde hair cascades over the edge of the bed, so long it could touch the ground if she slid towards me another inch or so.

My ears burning, I pull clothes out of my suitcase in silence. I know I've been sheltered, but I didn't think my question was that funny. I have no desire for my mom to pull a Mrs. Barry on me and forbid me from hanging out with my cousin so soon after getting here. Anne of Green Gables is one of my favorite books, but I've always felt more of a kinship with the rule-following Diana Barry than Anne Shirley.

I glance out the window to the house next door. Will Romeo be invited to the party? I don't know if he and Rosie are still friends, he hasn't mentioned her in his letters for a couple of years. I never asked why, afraid of bringing up a painful subject. But I know he still lives next door, the letter I sent him last month had my old address.

When Rosie's laughter dies down, I peer at her. "It wasn't that funny, but my question still stands."

Rosie rolls back over onto her stomach, looking me in the eye. "Honestly, probably not. Tyson pulled enough shady business when he was in high school that my parents are smarter than to leave any alcohol around where we can get at it." She shrugs. "It doesn't matter. If anyone will bring anything over it'll be Steph and Tia. Their mom doesn't care what they do."

"You won't get in trouble?" I can't help asking. The party is two days away and I'm already nervous. "I don't want you to get grounded or anything."

"I've never been grounded before." Rosie smirks.

Have I found a rule-following partner in non-crime?

My hopes are dashed when Rosie winks. "I'm too smart to get caught."

CHAPTER FOUR

Ninth Grade

ROMEO,

So how did it go with Angelica? Did you use daffodils like I said? Or did you go with red roses? I know roses mean "love," but I think daffodils are more romantic. How can you not swoon over flowers that mean "the sun is always shining when I'm with you?" Did she swoon? Or was it more of an Ava situation and you ended up with a faceful of flowers? You have to admit that getting flowers thrown in your face is probably more pleasant than hot chocolate.

Well, just like I guessed, I was stuck inside the embassy while everyone else was out at the Great Union Day celebration. I did get to watch the parade from a balcony, but my dad wouldn't let me go out to see what it was like. There were fireworks and dancers and I could barely see any of it. Bucharest is turning out to be as big a disappointment as Cyprus was. At least here the beach isn't tempting me.

One day, I'm going to come back to all the places we've lived and I'll finally get to *see* them. Be a real tourist, with a giant camera, okay maybe not too giant, I don't want to make myself an easy target, but a camera, my passport and a backpack. That's it. I want to be able to go wherever I want, whenever I want. No parents saying "no Juliet," or "it's not safe Juliet." I want to *live*, I want to explore. I want to try all the weird foods and go to all the shrines and temples and see what makes each place special.

I guess for now I'll have to content myself with reading my books and imagining your adventures, wooing a new girl every week. I tried to make a list of the girls you've told me about over the last two years, am I missing anyone? Sarah Dempsey, Marissa, Lily, Claire #1, Melody, Melanie, Melissa (how on earth did you keep all those M names straight? How many times did you call them the wrong name? Oh! Is that what happened with Melissa, is that why she got mad?), Haley, Chloe, Claire #2, Sarah Dempsey again, Heather, Melody again, Claire #3 (what is with you and Claires?), and Laci. I feel like I must be missing some but I can't remember.

Do you keep a list too, or am I just weird? I like to keep track of things, you never know when it might be important later. I've got a list of all the places we've lived and what order I want to go back and visit them. I even organized them into a calendar, so I can go when there are certain festivals that I want to experience. If you're going to tease me about my list of places to visit, just remember that I have a list of every girl you've had a crush on. I could blackmail you too!

Bored in Bucharest,
JULES

JULES,

Geez, way to kick a guy when he's down. That list is just mean. I can't believe you would go for the low blow like that. What kind of weirdo word is "woo"? Wooing is for old-timey dudes in tights and pointy shoes. And no, the flowers were not a success. Turns out that daffodils are hard to come by in December so I gave Angelica a sprig of mistletoe instead and she went and held it over Perry's head.

Perry!

I'm officially giving up girls if they're going to go for that a-hole over me. He wouldn't know how to kiss a girl if there was a step-by-step instruction manual. Is there a manual? I feel like I should send it to you, since it doesn't sound like you'll ever get a chance to practice before you're thirty.

I think it's cool that you want to travel one day. I wouldn't know where to go or what to do—I've never been outside the US. The farthest I've ever gone was to Arizona for a baseball tournament. Oak Hills would be super boring to you.

Ugh. Now you've got me all depressed, thinking about that list of girls who've rejected me and how I've never been anywhere cool. Thanks Jules, way to be a friend.

I'm too depressed to write now. I think I'll go throw myself off the roof instead. Or maybe I'll play Xbox until I make myself dinner.

—ROME

p.s. I was kidding about the roof thing.

p.p.s. You forgot to add Angelica, Bridget and Naomi to the list. And Chrissy.

CHAPTER FIVE

Juliet

"ARE PARTIES always this loud?" I lean close to Rosie from our perch at the top of the stairs. She just grins and rolls her eyes at me. "And what's with the masks? You didn't say anything about masks."

Rosie rolls her eyes again and points at a group of boys just visible through the open front door. "Marcus and his idiot friends have been handing them out to everyone as they walk in. The masks were not my idea."

"Rosie! The masks are so cool. It's like, romantic and shit." A tallish girl with dark brown hair and a beautiful bronze complexion stumbles up the stairs toward us. "Who's this?" She glares at me, her eyes bloodshot and hazy, but sharp enough to see that I'm new.

"Chill, Tia. This is my cousin Juliet. She's staying with us for the summer."

Tia looks me up and down, eyeing my white sundress and wrinkling her nose. "Hmph."

"Okay Judgey McJudgerson, take it down a notch." Rosie's voice is laced with annoyance at Tia's words. "Juliet, Tia. Tia, Juliet."

I stick my hand out to be polite, even if there is no way I want to be friends with this girl. She knows nothing about me except my name and she's already being mean. "Hi, nice to meet you. Tia's a beautiful name, is it short for anything?"

"It's short for Gamzatti, but no one calls me that." Tia sniffs at me. "My mom was a real ballet-nut, lucky me."

"Oh, we saw a production of La Bayadere in Istanbul once, it was beautiful." Maybe there's someone nice under Tia's attitude? "Have you ever seen it?"

Tia looks me up and down again, pulling a face as my question sinks in. "Uh no. Ballet is for dorks."

Well, I guess Tia and I aren't destined to be bosom-buddies.

"Where are your masks?" Tia turns to Rosie. "I would have thought you'd have the best ones."

Rosie looks around, everyone else inside the house has some kind of mask on, except for us. "I'll get them in a minute. Have you seen Marcus? Did his sister come?"

"I haven't seen Melody. Why?" Tia narrows her eyes at Rosie.

A girl who can only be Tia's sister comes up the stairs behind her. Her dark hair is pulled up in a braided crown on her head, her mask of purple and black swirls covers her eyes, but the way she stands next to Tia, the set of their shoulders matching, she can't be anything but related. "Who's this?" She smacks the gum in her mouth as she talks but smiles, a little friendlier than Tia.

"Steph, this is Juliet, my cousin. Juliet, this is Tia's sister Steph."

"Hi." I'm more cautious this time, not offering anything else they can use to judge me. I'm well aware of how strange my upbringing was compared to these girls. I've lived my whole life surrounded by adults. My only real friends my cousin, a pen pal I've never met, and the occasional other kid trapped in the same weird life as me.

I wonder if Romeo is here? He could be one of the boys downstairs and I'd never know—we've never exchanged pictures or talked about what we look like. It never occurred to me that I'd want to know. In my mind Romeo's become an amalgamation of Gilbert Blythe, Henry Tilney and Charles Bingley—my three favorite book boyfriends. But not one of the broody ones, he'd never be a Darcy or an Edward Cullen. I know from his letters he's a terrible flirt. Terrible, as in he can't stop doing it, and also doesn't seem to be very successful at it. I know he's funny, cares about his friends, and is much smarter than anyone gives him credit for.

"So you're the cousin who lives all over the place?" Steph asks. "How come you're stuck here with us? I wouldn't be in Oak Hills if I could be somewhere else."

"My dad got stationed in a part of Turkey that's kind of unstable right now. They sent me to stay with Uncle Chuck and Aunt Cathy for the summer. If it settles down I can go back, but if not, I'll stay here for senior year too."

"Cool, whatever. Rosie, the boys are looking for you."

Rosie blows out an annoyed breath. "The boys? Or one boy in particular?"

Steph and Tia share a look and shrug. "We were told to tell you 'the boys.'"

"That means he thinks he's being cute. Dammit. I was hoping he would have moved on by now. At least that means he's in a good mood." Rosie shakes her head and puffs out another big breath. "Hang on…" She turns to look at me. "Oh, this is perfect. Jules, you can do it."

I'm so lost—I have no idea who or what they're talking about. "Um…I can do what?"

"*You* can go distract them." Rosie smiles, like needing someone to distract the boys is a normal thing. Or easy for that matter.

"Um, I think I'm the worst choice for that. I don't know how to flirt. And why do you need them to be distracted?"

"Ugh, Jules, just do it, please?" She turns her puppy dog eyes on me and I cave.

"Wait! You guys need masks. Don't go anywhere." Steph and Tia disappear back down the stairs.

"Rosie, what's going on?" I cross my arms and glare.

Instead of explaining, Rosie grabs me by the hand and pulls me into her bedroom, closing the door behind me. "It's this guy. He has a crush on me, but I don't like him that way. He's a total flirt. He'll be over it in a week if I can just distract him. Trust me, I know what a player he is. Besides…" She cuts off before finishing that sentence. I wait a moment to see if she's going to say anything else. When she doesn't, I sigh, sitting on her baby blue bed.

"So you want me to distract some guy who likes you but you don't like him?"

Rosie nods, like it's that easy.

"Okay, but how am I supposed to do that? I've never talked to a boy in my life."

Rosie grins. "For starters, don't talk about ballet or the opera or whatever. No guy is going to be into that. Just smile and laugh at his jokes. Trust me, this guy will talk enough for both of you. I swear, he never shuts up."

A knock on her door interrupts us. Steph sticks her head in. "Benny gave me these for you." She holds out two masks. One is blue with peacock feathers in a crown across the top. The other is covered with white feathers, gold glitter splashed thick on one side and fading to nothing on the other.

Rosie hands me the white mask, to match my dress. She puts hers on and stands next to me in the full-length mirror on one side of her room. We share the same blonde hair as our mothers, although my shoulder length bob is a lighter shade than hers. Rosie has a couple inches on my perfectly average five-five frame, but my legs are longer and my boobs just a little bigger.

"Rosie, I don't think I can do this." I stare at myself in the mirror. The white sundress I borrowed from Rosie hangs loose from my shoulders to the middle of my thighs. It's not form-fitting, but it is pretty short—my dad would never have let me leave the house in it.

"You'll be fine. Didn't you say you wanted to be a normal high schooler? Well, now's your chance. What could possibly be more normal than flirting with boys?" She squeezes my shoulders. "I need you to distract him from me, Jules. I will never like him the way he wants, but he's my friend, and I don't want it to get weird."

"Why don't you tell him that?" I don't understand why my brash and bold cousin is trying to take the sneaky way out. "This isn't like you Rosie."

She sighs and glances at the closed door. "Jules, please? I just want things to go back to normal, where he's my annoying, over-dramatic friend and nothing more. I swear, he'll be over it the next time he meets a pretty girl. And then it won't ruin our summer."

I lean my head on her shoulder. "Well, when you put it like that…Fine."

Rosie hustles me down the stairs before I can change my mind, nodding and smiling at everyone, until we get to a group of three guys hanging near the front door. They turn as we approach, each of them wearing their own mask.

"Well, hello, hello," the tallest one says. What I can see of his hair is dark blonde, a little long but stylishly mussed. His crisp short-sleeve, button down shirt and shorts fit him perfectly, just tight enough to show his broad shoulders and trim waist. His arms are tanned, like he spends a lot of time outside, and bright blue eyes stand out against his bronzed skin.

I swallow down a squeak and smile, my eyes flitting to the other two guys standing with him.

Almost as tall as the Nordic specimen is a young man who might be Japanese, or maybe Korean. I can't tell with the red and orange mask he's wearing, but it doesn't hide his razor sharp cheekbones or pillowy lips. Not as broad as the other two, he's wiry and lean, rather than muscular. "Hi, I'm Benny." He holds out a hand and I shake it, still silent, my lips falling open under the gaze of these three.

The Nordic one throws one arm over Benny and the other arm over their friend, grinning beneath his mask. "And who do we have the pleasure of meeting? Or are you just here to admire us? Admiration is a perfectly acceptable answer, by the way. Benny here isn't used to it, he did a Neville Longbottom this year and hasn't gotten used to his new level of hotness." He laughs and holds tight when Benny struggles out from under his arm.

The third guy still hasn't spoken, but his green eyes never leave my face, brilliant even in the shadowy depths of his solid black mask. My cheeks turn warm under his silent gaze and I want to look anywhere but at him. I fiddle with the long gold chain necklace I'm wearing instead.

The blonde clears his throat. "I'm Marcus, by the way." I tear my gaze away from their silent companion to offer a small smile. Now that I'm standing here, like a lamb before the wolves, it occurs to me that Rosie never told me who she was avoiding.

Marcus asks me if I want a drink, but every cell in my body is tuned to the silent third member of their party. Who is this boy? Why do I feel like I know him, like he knows me? He hasn't said a word, but his eyes burn into me, speaking to something beyond my senses.

He's dressed all in black, matching his mask. He can't be the one Rosie is avoiding. She said he was an incorrigible flirt, which Marcus has been this whole time. I should go with them to get a drink, but I'm pinned to the spot, unable to tear myself away from the devil-in-black's piercing eyes.

CHAPTER SIX

Romeo

AN ANGEL is standing in front of me.

How else can I describe her?

A delicate chin and full lips peek from beneath her mask. The white feathers on it hide everything but her wide, innocent gray-blue eyes. Her white dress, white blonde hair, and the feathery mask only enhance the angelic look. Words vanish from my brain and I drink her in.

My heart thuds in my chest. Did it ever truly beat before this angel fell from heaven to grace us with her presence? She has captured me in a spell and I don't want to break free. Nothing else matters except getting her to speak to me, smile at me, tell me her name.

Marcus is talking but I don't hear a word he says, every cell in my body waiting for her to speak.

"We're getting a drink, do you want something?" Benny bumps my arm. I shake my head at the same time the angel shakes hers. She watches Benny and Marcus walk away, biting her bottom lip, a worried wrinkle pulling at her forehead.

An idea pops into my mind. There's a chance she won't catch the reference, but for some reason, I'm convinced this angel has read Shakespeare more than once.

I dredge up Romeo's lines from the depths of my brain, clearing my throat twice before I can speak. "I feel as if I shouldn't touch you with unclean hands. An angel like you doesn't belong in a place like this."

Her mouth drops open with a gasp and I hurry to butcher the next lines.

"Someone could spill something on you, even if all you do is stand. I'd hate to see you hurt—unless I can make it better with a kiss?'

Without warning, she takes my hand, turning it over in hers, tracing my palm with one long finger. Electricity shoots up my arm, setting my heart on fire. "I think your hand is fine, you worry too much. But if you wanted to greet me properly, you would do this." She holds up her hand and presses her palm to mine. "This is how the pilgrims greet the monks, with a touch. Palm to palm is the closest you'll get to a kiss."

Dumbstruck that she's going along with it," I blurt out the next line, turning my hand to capture her fingers in mine. "So you've never used those delicious lips, or have you done that too?"

The angel tries to pull away but I hold tight, bringing her hand up so I can press my lips to the top of her hand. If I'm going to make an ass of myself with this Shakespeare shit, I'm going to get a kiss out of it at least. Memorizing lines is hard work.

"I've used my lips for lots of things, silly—speaking, eating, prayer." Again, she tugs her hand but I hold tight, pulling her closer. Who is she?

I go for broke. "Well then, dear angel, if monks and pilgrims greet palm to palm, does that mean we let our lips do what hands do? Isn't that a kind of prayer, one that keeps a young man like me from despair?" This conversation is over the top, even for me, but I haven't read *Romeo and Juliet* a dozen times for nothing. I'm named after the dude, of course I've read it—Leonardo DiCaprio is obviously my favorite version.

A laugh bubbles up from her lips and it takes everything in me not to kiss her. I know she's laughing at me, but for once I don't care. Instead of making me feel like a clown, her laughter fills me with a thousand flames.

"The monks and priests would be scandalized by you. I'm shocked for their sake." She giggles out the words and I smirk. All that time I spent memorizing Romeo and Juliet's first meeting from the play has finally come in handy. I told Marcus it would.

Leaning in close, I whisper in her ear. "Then hold still while I 'pray' and a kiss I shall take." I sound like an idiot, but it's working. The angel is stock-still while I brush my lips across hers. It's just a feathery touch—I wouldn't even count it as a kiss—but the tingle of her lips against mine has my brain short-circuiting.

"Romeo!"

Rosie shrieking my name from across the room shatters the spell between us. The angel jerks back with a gasp. "Romeo?"

I rub a hand at the back of my neck. Now that I've come back to Earth, I take in the silence of the house and the way everyone is staring at me and my angel. "Uh, yeah?" Before my angel can speak, Rosie comes crashing through the crowd of people and grabs her by the arm, pulling her behind her back.

"Jesus, Jules, I said distract him, not make out with him!" My angel, Jules apparently, hides behind Rosie, but not before she sends a shocked look in my direction, muttering something I can't hear to Rosie.

"Marcus?" Rosie laughs. "Pfft, I can handle Marcus." She whirls to face me, poking a hard finger in my chest. "You stay away from her, cretin. You forget how well I know you. I won't let you anywhere near my cousin."

Cousin?

"Jules...Juliet? That's your cousin Juliet?" I've written it a hundred times over the years, never admitting to anyone how much I looked forward to her letters. The letters that started as a bet I lost to Rosie but became a place where I could be myself. No acting, no pretense, no vying for attention. The faceless Juliet was my solace when life here was shit, her loneliness in the midst of an exotic country mirroring my own loneliness in the midst of my popularity.

I wasn't far wrong when I called her an angel.

"Uh, hi?" She peeks out from behind Rosie, pulling the mask off her face. Her fairy-like features are a more delicate version of Rosie. "Hang on...*Romeo* was who you...?" Wide-eyed, Juliet turns to me, the shock on her face turning to hurt. "You added Rosie to your list? No way, not cool." Her fingers touch her lips, as if she can still feel the same tingle that I do.

Rosie's arms are crossed, head cocked to the side. "What list?"

CHAPTER SEVEN

Juliet

"UMMMM, NO list. There's no list, right Juliet?" Just hearing him say my name has my heart racing. Or maybe that's the death stare that Rosie's giving us both. Romeo holds up his hands and takes a step back, plastering a charming smile on his face. "Anyway, it's nice to finally meet you Juliet. Welcome to Oak Hills." He sidesteps Rosie, never turning his back on her, smart boy.

I stare at him as he moves through the crowd. *That's* Romeo? My unexpected friend, the only person who knows how lonely my life is beneath the glamor of living abroad? "What list is he talking about Jules? We need to decontaminate your mouth if his slimy lips have touched yours."

I don't have a chance to argue before Rosie pulls me up the stairs and into her bathroom. "Rinse." She points to a bottle of mouthwash on the counter. "I'm serious, I won't be held responsible if you end up with mono or something from him."

Knowing it's pointless to argue, I grab the bottle and take a swig, the sharp sting of the alcohol making tears prick my eyes. Rosie watches me like a hawk until I've spat it out in the sink. "Happy now?" I wipe my mouth on a towel.

Rosie huffs. "What list?"

Drat, I thought she'd let it go. "It's just an old joke from our letters. It's nothing, I promise." When Rosie doesn't move to let me pass, I lean back against the bathroom counter. "I teased him about having a crush on a new girl in every letter, so I made a list and kept it updated."

"If you knew what a flirt he was, why did you kiss him?" Rosie eyes me. "I'm not jealous, if that's what you're thinking," she adds when I hesitate to answer.

"I didn't know it was *him*. We didn't actually kiss you know, it was just…breathing really close together." I wince at my lame description but it's true. There was just the barest touching of skin to skin.

Rosie looks doubtful. "That looked like kissing to me. Gross, Jules." Rosie shudders. "He's like my brother. That's so disgusting."

Now it's my turn to bristle. "Okay, easy there. First of all, there was no, uh, lip pressure so it doesn't count as a kiss. I'm *not* letting my first kiss be that." I wave my arms around. "And secondly, enough with the grossness, you're making me feel like a creeper."

Rosie offers me the bottle of Listerine again but I push it away, laughing. "Nah, I'm good. Trust me, I won't make that mistake again. I know Romeo too well to fall into that trap a second time." I push past her and make my way downstairs.

Now that I know who it is Rosie's avoiding, it makes sense. He is her neighbor after all, if things get awkward, it would make for a crappy summer. And knowing how fast Romeo moves from crush to crush, I understand why she thinks distracting him with a shiny new toy is better than confronting him. I know for a fact she's never liked him that way.

I make my way down the stairs and back into the party. Someone turned on music and people are all over the house, spilling out into the backyard through the big sliding glass doors across from the stairs. Tia and Steph are in one corner with Marcus, laughing and passing something between them.

I avert my eyes from whatever it is they're doing and scan the room again. Benny and Romeo are talking to a very pretty girl. The yellow sundress she's wearing stands out against her dark skin, a cascade of box braids hanging down her back, that swing with each movement of her head. Her shoulders and arms are muscular and toned. I glance at my own stick arms as jealousy flashes through me. Benny's eyes track every movement she makes, even as Romeo dominates the conversation, his arms waving wildly above his head, his animated face pulling into ridiculous expressions.

Since I don't know anyone else, I make my way to them. "Hey." Gosh, I'm so lame.

But Romeo smiles his charming smile at me—nope I'm not going to let my heart flip flop like that when I see the famous dimple in his cheek—and shifts to make space for me. "Hey. Nikki, this is Juliet, Rosie's cousin. Juliet, this is Nikki."

"You're the one who lives in Europe, right?" Her voice is soft and I relax, glad she isn't trying to intimidate me like the other girls.

I nod. "Yeah, kind of. Mostly around Turkey and the Mediterranean, since that's my dad's specialty." I chat with Nikki, answering her questions while Benny and Romeo hover, listening in and laughing with us.

If this is what a real high school party is like, I suppose I was worried for nothing. There's no one dancing or acting crazy, I don't smell weed or anything besides slightly sweaty bodies.

"Do you girls want a drink?" Romeo asks in a lull in the conversation. When we nod, he and Benny head outside, leaving Nikki and I alone. We've been standing near the kitchen counter this whole time, leaning against the countertop facing the rest of the house. Nikki hops up on a stool tucked underneath it, offering me the one next to her.

"My feet are killing me. I had rehearsal after school." Nikki sighs, pulling her orange mask off and massaging her shoulder with one hand while I perch on the other stool. I struggle to get on it without flashing anyone, but in the end, I sort of half sit on it and figure it's good enough. Nikki watches me struggle with a friendly smile. "Not used to wearing such a short dress are you?"

"How did you know?" I pull my own mask off with a cringe. Great, the one person I thought might be a friend and she already knows how awkward I am. I avoid looking at her, running my fingers over the soft feathers on the front of my mask instead.

"It just takes practice to get all the way on without flashing anyone." She laughs and I glance at her. There's no judgement in her eyes, no smirk because I'm a dork who can't even get on a stool like a normal person. I can't help joining in, still fiddling with the elastic string of my mask.

"Yeah. My parents are a little, um, overprotective. We've been living in Turkey for the last year so it was always easiest to wear something long, then I knew no one would get upset with me. I have quite a collection of long skirts, even though I kind of hate wearing them." I pluck at the fabric of my dress. "I borrowed this from Rosie." More like she threatened to cut the hems off all my clothes if I didn't wear it.

"Here you go, ladies." Red solo cups, just like in all the TV shows and movies I've watched, are thrust toward me and Nikki. Taking it, I peer inside. Red punch swirls around, the sweet scent of it floating up as I sniff.

Romeo leans in to whisper in my ear. "It's virgin, I promise. Steph tried to doctor it but I didn't let her." At my questioning look, he shrugs. "I remember things, Angel." His breath tickles my ear, the only possible explanation for why goosebumps prickle the back of my neck. It has nothing to do with how good he smells. Or the adorable way his mask is shoved up on his forehead.

Stop it. Stop it right now Juliet. This is *Romeo*. You know better than this. He's a flirt. A player. He loves the chase. How many letters have you read from him where all he talks about is a new pretty girl? He's a Wickham or a Willoughby, not Mr. Darcy and certainly no Gilbert Blythe. I push aside the thrill of having a boy standing so near and pay attention to the story Nikki is telling us about her dance rehearsal today.

When she and Benny get into a discussion about some K-pop band I've never heard of, I pull on my best, bravest, diplomatic self and turn to Romeo. "So. Rosie, huh?"

The tips of his ears turn pink while he hides his face by taking a sip of his drink. "It just happened."

I eye him. "I know you better than that. You've written to me about every girl you've ever met, and never a word about Rosie. So either—she's the one you've really wanted this whole time, in which case I'll help. Even though she doesn't like you that way and you haven't got a snowball's chance in H-E-double hockey sticks." He opens his mouth to protest but I keep talking. "Or, this is another one of your struck-by-lightning infatuations and I will break your kneecaps if you so much as attempt to flirt with her."

"You can't say 'hell' but you can threaten bodily harm? You, Angel, are an odd duck." Irritated that he's laughing at me, I stick one fist on my hip, the other wiggling my cup in agitation. Romeo stops, looks at me, then bursts out laughing again. "Jules, you look like an angry pixie."

I glower more.

"Intimidation is not your forte. Stick to being smarter than everyone else in the room."

"Romeo, I'm serious." I debate sharing what Rosie told me earlier. My instinct is to be protective of my cousin, even though she doesn't need my help. But Romeo has been my friend, in a weird long-distance kind of way, for a long time and I don't want him to get hurt either.

It has nothing to do with the fireworks that went off in my belly when his lips brushed against mine.

I swear.

"Jules, I don't know. It just kind of hit me in the car the other day." He shrugs, but can't hide the way the blush on his ears is creeping up his neck. "She looked really pretty when we were driving to school, that's all."

"So, this isn't some long-held secret infatuation? You haven't been pining for her for years?" I want to make sure I'm right before I say anything. I believed Rosie when she said she would never like Romeo as more than a friend, but if he's really loved her for a long time I would be the first one in line to help him win her over. Maybe all those girls he's flirted with have been a distraction because he's secretly in love with Rosie. Doesn't she deserve to be loved like that?

I push down the hurt that creeps into my heart that Romeo could have been using me like all those other girls.

He shakes his head. "No Jules, I have not been *pining*. Rosie's always been like a sister to me. I just couldn't help wondering what it would be like, that's all." His green eyes are clear and honest, looking straight into mine.

"You're sure?" Am I insisting because I want to protect my cousin, or because I want to protect myself?

Romeo holds my gaze and nods. "I'm sure."

And for some reason, I believe him.

CHAPTER EIGHT

Romeo

MY BRAIN is having a hard time reconciling that this beautiful, ethereal waif of a girl is the same Juliet who told me exactly how to pack my bag for a tournament weekend—the queen of practical planning and triple-checking your work. She looks like she should live in a forest surrounded by flowers and small animals who come when she sings.

The same girl who teases me endlessly about my ability to fall in and out of love at the drop of a hat is the innocent fairy looking at me through her lashes? I don't know why, but I pictured Jules more like Rosie, a little tougher, a little more physically intimidating to match the brains I know she has.

She pins me with those gray-blue eyes. "You promise?"

"Rosie's forgotten." Her eyes narrow and I trip over my tongue to correct my mistake. "Not *forgotten* forgotten, but any idea that she might be more than a friend is gone. Poof. Vanished. It's stupid." I grab the back of my neck and grin down at her. "Besides, she'd snap me in two if I actually tried anything."

Juliet's laugh rings out, louder than expected. "Well, then. I'm glad to have saved you from the pain of being snapped in two. And glad I saved Rosie from the trouble of having to bury your body."

Someone jostles me from behind and the smell of too generously applied body spray assaults my nose. "Hello there." A familiar arm appears in my peripheral vision. "I'm Perry, nice to meet you."

Perry St. Clair has a punchable face. It's a handsome face, but the condescending and conniving attitude behind it makes it impossible to want to do anything but send a well-placed fist through it. The only reason no one's done it yet is because his dad is the principal of our school and he's our teammate. You don't punch teammates in the face, no matter how much they deserve it. Not if you want to stay on the team.

Jules gives him a suspicious look, before extending her own hand to shake. "Hi, I'm Juliet."

Perry hooks an arm around my neck, jerking me in to knuckle the top of my head, knocking my mask off and to the floor. "Romeo and Juliet, huh? Maybe I should steal you away from him so we can avoid tragedy." From the headlock he has me in I can't see his face, but I can hear the leer in his voice and my blood boils. Jules is my friend, dammit, and I'm not letting Perry fucking St. Clair get his disgusting hands on her.

"No one is stealing me, claiming me, or doing anything of the sort." Juliet says before I can get free of Perry's stupid bicep. "I can make my own decisions, thanks." She takes a sip from her cup, eyeing Perry and me over the edge. "Besides, I already know Romeo is a flirt who falls in love with every pretty face he sees."

I slap a hand over my heart and gasp, finally free from the headlock. Perry chuckles and I punch him in the stomach, a little harder than necessary. Jules cocks her head and smirks.

"I see you're not denying it." She turns her gaze to Perry and looks him up and down. "Perry, I can tell, is the kind of guy who makes a lot of promises that don't go anywhere." Perry doesn't react, still clutching his stomach and wheezing.

I whistle low and long. "Damn Jules, when did you get so observant? You've been here for what, a couple of days?"

She grins at me. "Two days. But I've known *you* for a lot longer than that."

Perry straightens up and starts to laugh at me, but she knocks the wind out of him with her next words. "And I saw Perry coming from a mile away. It's the hair. The perfect swoop gives him away. There's no way a swoop like that can be achieved in less than twenty minutes. *I* don't even take that long to do my hair."

Now it's my turn to laugh as Perry's hand goes to his perfectly gelled hair. I step closer to her, not sure if I'm shielding her from Perry or if she's the true north to my magnetic personality. I bump her shoulder with mine. "So, you prefer the shaggy look to the preppy. Noted."

She smiles up at me and my heart flips over in my chest. I don't know what this is that I'm feeling for her, it's new and strange, but I know that I'll do everything in my power to protect her from an asshole like Perry. She deserves someone who's as perfect as she is, someone smart, someone who doesn't screw up like me and won't use her to make themselves look good like him.

"Whatever. See you around, Juliet." Perry takes off with a backwards glance at her, his eyes narrowed as he looks her up and down one more time. I don't trust him, but I'm glad he's gone for now. It's only when he's out of sight that Jules lets out an enormous breath and sags on her feet. That's when the shaking cup in her hand catches my eye.

"Are you okay?" I take the cup and steer her out the door into Rosie's backyard. There's still a crowd of people back here, but at least there's no lack of oxygen from pompous assholes like Perry hogging it all with their big heads. "Jules?"

She sits down in one of the deck chairs, hands flapping uselessly at her pink cheeks. "Ohmygodohmygodohmygodohmygod. I can't believe I just said that. *I* just said that. Me. I told a stranger he was vain. To his face. To his actual smug face. With words. With out loud, audible words. Oh my gosh. My mother will kill me. I'm dead. I'm dead. *Dead*, dead. Like actual dead, not just figurative dead. Do you think Rosie has a coffin? I can never show my face again. That's it. I'm going back to Turkey. Or maybe I'll find an all-girls boarding school and I'll just go there. I can't say something stupid and rude about a boy's hair if there are no boys, right?" She stops to suck in a breath and chokes on it, her coughing turning into gasps for air.

I thump her on the back, not too hard since she's so tiny, and look around the yard. "Hang on, I'll be right back. Don't tell off anyone else before I get back."

She gapes at me, face red and eyes leaking as she coughs. I hurry off to the cooler on the other side of the deck and rummage through the cans of soda for a water bottle. I pull one from the icy water and pop the cap as I speed walk back to Jules.

She takes it from me, sipping until she gets her breath under control. I stand there, useless, until she manages a full breath without coughing. Squatting in front of her, I take the bottle when she can't seem to decide what to do with it and she runs her fingers under her eyes to wipe away the tears. "Thanks."

"No problem. You okay now? Panic attack over?"

She smacks my knee and only my years of squatting in this exact position with my catcher's mitt keep me from falling backwards at her touch. There's that zing between us again, my heart stopping for an instant before starting again. I don't understand it. I've been in love so many times before and I've never felt anything like this.

"Don't tease, panic attacks are a real thing. That was regular old hyperventilating at the idea of my mother seeing me now. Talking to a boy. No, *boys.*" She emphasizes the plural and winces. "Not just talking, but being rude. And you can see my knees." Her voice drops to a whisper with her last words and I struggle to hold back a laugh.

"Ah, yes. Knees. Very scandalous, those knobbly things." I pat one for emphasis, which is a mistake. Her skin is soft and my fingers linger, dancing just above the bend of her knee. I drop my gaze, watching myself trace circles on her skin. Juliet murmurs above me, but I don't hear her words, mesmerized by the smooth, creamy skin beneath my touch.

"…let lips do what hands do…" Her words penetrate the spell I'm under and I glance up, grinning. I press a kiss to the end of her knee and push to my feet.

"I believe your reputation as a good girl is still intact, fair Juliet. Your brazen display of ankles and knees haven't besmirched your honor yet, nor has standing up for yourself. Besides, Perry needs the wind let out of his ego on a regular basis or else he has to drive with the windows down 'cause his head won't fit inside. Come on." I pull Jules to her feet, letting go once she's up, even though I don't want to.

"I'm nervous." Her whispered words surprise me.

"But you were chatting with Nikki and Benny earlier, you didn't seem nervous to me." I run a hand through my hair so I don't grab her hand again, and step towards the rest of the party.

Jules smiles. "I was being Anne."

"Who?"

She ducks her head, biting her lip. "Anne Shirley?"

"Who?" I have no idea who or what she's talking about, but something tells me I should from our letters. "Is that a character from a book?"

Juliet's laugh sends heat racing up the back of my neck. "*Anne of Green Gables*? It's only one of my favorites."

The heat fades from my neck and I cover my embarrassment with a smirk. "Don't you remember? If it doesn't have pictures, I'm not interested."

CHAPTER NINE

Tenth Grade

JULIET,

Can you explain girls to me?

Let me explain. On Saturday, I was with my boys at the lake, relaxing, having a good time. B-Boy brought his dad's machete, which was so cool, and we were hacking at shit stuff 'cause we were going to make a fire to roast hot dogs and make s'mores later.

Hot dogs roasted over a fire just hit different, you know? I swear I could eat an entire packet of hot dogs if they were roasted over a fire.

Anyway, while we were hunting for wood (heh, *wood*), we met this other group of sophomore girls who were hanging out farther down the shore from us. Not going to lie, Jules, the one girl was super hot, but her friends…not so much. So B-Boy, Monkey, and I were tossing branches into a pile and yes, I admit I was flexing a little extra, I've been working out with the boys and I wanted to see if they noticed (spoiler: they noticed).

These girls came and watched us doing it. We were all talking, having a good time, you know, the usual, and I was thinking maybe I had a chance with the hot one. She kept watching me, you know? And every time I looked she would wink or smile or something. There was definite flirting going on.

Monkey noticed her too and started picking up heavier and heavier logs, so I did too. Then he pulled a freaking Captain America move and broke one in half with his bare hands. B-Boy was using his machete to hack up some wood but I didn't have a knife. So hot girl, her name was Claire, by the way, was starting to watch Monkey more than me, and well, that's just not acceptable.

My name is *Romeo*, for crying out loud. It's only natural for girls to fall in love with me, right?

I step up my game and grab a bigger piece, then Monkey gets one that's bigger. I'm sure you can start to guess where this is going. Finally, I grab the biggest piece I can find and start to break it in two. And I don't know exactly how it happened. Maybe it was my inner Hulk coming out. Or maybe it was the fact that right as I tried to break it I saw Claire lean in to whisper something in Monkey's ear—even though she was eyeing me like I was chocolate cake and she was on her period—but I ripped that piece of wood in half.

You've seen the gif right? Of Captain America ripping the log in half? That was me, Jules. Okay, I maaaaay have screamed a little more than I grunted as I did it, and I may have peed myself just a drip, but you would too if you ripped a log in half.

It was only after I did it that I felt the pain. When I tell you it was the most excruciating pain I've ever felt in my life I'm not exaggerating. Now I understand why they use this as a threat in mafia movies. I am never going to piss off the Bratva. What hurt so bad, you ask?

I looked down at the branch in one hand and MY FINGERNAIL WAS HANGING FROM THE BARK! My whole, entire, fingernail. I ripped my own goddamn fingernail off and it hurt worse than getting kneed in the nuts. Okay maybe not worse, but equal to. It really depends on how hard you hit the nuts.

So I'm rolling on the ground, in agony, when someone touches my back. Was it Claire? Nope. She had her face buried in Monkey's shoulder and he was laughing at me over the top of her head. Some best friend, right?

Long story short, it was not the girl I was showing off for who came to my rescue with a bandage, it was one of her not pretty friends. Explain to me, Jules, why is it that the prettiest ones make you work so hard for it, and then when you bust yourself up over them, turn to the guy who didn't do as much? Huh?

I don't understand you women.

But my finger is okay and the nail is already growing back. It's a great story, even if Rosie thinks I'm an idiot for doing it in the first place.

Hulk out.

DEAR ROMEO,

Sometimes I forget that you're a real person. Not because your stories are so ridiculous, or because I forget about you. Promise!

But all of my best friends are characters in books. Because honestly, who else is going to be my friend? I'm the only fifteen-year-old girl living in our embassy right now. There are a few younger kids, but most of the staff who have teenagers send them off to boarding school for high school, so they don't get dragged around the world like me.

But Mom insists on homeschooling me herself, because no boarding school is going to be strict enough for her. So, I'm stuck here. Sometimes I feel like Rapunzel, trapped in my tower. Except I don't have long hair.

So, I read about all my 'friends' lives, including yours. And sometimes I forget that you're not just a character made up by an author, but you're a real, live, actual person. Is it weird that I consider you my friend, even though we've never met and maybe never will?

It's probably for the best that we never meet in real life—with our names we'd be doomed to a tragic end. Better to play it safe, right?

But I love your stories! I can just picture you, Monkey and B-Boy showing off for all those girls. Did you ever actually ask them if they needed the firewood? Did you get to eat the hot dogs and s'mores you wanted? I've never had a s'more, but they sound delicious. My mom doesn't let me have any processed food.

One day, I'm going to try all the American food I've read about and never had like churros, soft pretzels, s'mores, and pizza. I mean, we have those things here, but I want to try them in America. It's been so long now I don't remember what they taste like. I do remember pizza from when I was little—pizza was amazing. Although, we get amazing pizza here too (how could we not?) it's not the same.

I'm making a Food list to add to my Travel list and your Girls list. Any other kinds of lists we should make? Maybe Experiences?

Stuck in Sicily,
JULIET

P.s. Is everything okay? That last letter was kind of scary. You didn't really take those pills, did you?

CHAPTER TEN

Juliet

"I DON'T THINK so, Rosie." I shake my head at the crop top and shorts she's pushing into my hands. "There's no way my parents would ever let me wear it."

"Yeah, but your parents aren't here and you're not in Turkey. Just try it on." She's smiling, but frustration laces her words. Probably because I've said the same thing at every outfit she's wanted me to try on. When Rosie suggested we go to the mall, I was envisioning smoothies and flipping through records, not trying on outfits at every clothing store we passed.

I realize now my idea of what a mall is like may be more influenced by the books and TV shows I've seen than reality. So instead of protesting, yet again, I close the dressing room door, pull on the high-waisted denim shorts and flowered crop top then step back out for Rosie's inspection.

"Happy?" I hold out my arms and do a spin before she can tell me to. The cold draft of the air conditioning tickles the back of my legs.

"You look fabulous. And that doesn't show nearly as much as you thought it would." Rosie points at my stomach, where the bottom of the shirt just brushes the top of the shorts. I have to admit she's right.

"Maybe. But my butt is not used to being out like this." I crane my neck to see over my shoulder at the offending body part, then tug the hem of the shorts in a vain attempt to cover my behind. "I can feel the breeze in places I'm not used to."

Laughing, Rosie shoves me into the dressing room to change back into my long skirt and shirt. By the time I emerge, she's nowhere to be seen. "Rosie?" I call, barely raising my voice. I scan the racks of clothing and shoes, eyes peeled for her blonde hair.

An explosion of laughter from the store entrance catches my attention. I spot her in a cluster with Romeo, Marcus, and Benny. She's punching Romeo on the arm, he looks sheepish but is grinning. Marcus has his head thrown back in a guffaw while Benny holds onto his shoulder, a fist in front of his face like he's trying to hold in his laugh. They look like they belong together, the four of them. Jealousy of their comfortable friendship surges through me. I want that.

"Jules!" Rosie bounces toward me, the boys following. "Okay, which ones are we buying?" She reaches for the hangers in my hand but I pull them away, looking for a rack to hang them on.

"I wasn't going to buy anything." I protest.

Rosie huffs. "Your dad gave you money, right?" When I nod she keeps going. "So why did he give you money if he didn't want you to spend it?"

"She has a point, you know." Romeo points a finger at me with a wink. "If we don't spend our parents' money, who will?"

The thought of spending money on whatever I feel like both intrigues and makes me nervous. My instinct tells me to check with my mom before buying something. I'd never admit to these guys that I've never gone clothes shopping without my mom to approve or disapprove of my choices. The only thing I buy without asking permission is books for my Kindle with gift cards I get for my birthday and Christmas.

But there is a wild feeling in my heart telling me to go for it, to buy the shorts that my father would never let me out of the house wearing, that my mother wouldn't have even let me try on in the first place.

"If it makes you feel better, you can leave them with me when you go back to Turkey, *if* you go back. Your parents will never know you bought them."

Romeo leans in close to whisper in my ear, sending goosebumps down my spine. "Your secret's safe with us, Angel."

Maybe it's the butterflies running riot in my belly, maybe it's the exasperation creeping into Rosie's expression, but that wild feeling takes over. "Okay, I'm buying them." I leave the clothes I'm not buying on a rack and march over to the register.

Someone steps close to me while the cashier rings me up, but I ignore them until a lipstick waves in my peripheral vision. "You should get this too." The deep voice startles me.

Whirling, I discover Marcus standing beside me, a bright red lipstick in his hand. "Why? I don't wear lipstick." The rude words pop out and I cringe. "Sorry."

He waves me off with a grin. "Maybe you should. You'd look hot." He winks, places the lipstick on the counter and wanders off, leaving me confused. Why on earth would Marcus care if I look hot? Does he...does he *like* me? Surely not.

I watch Marcus as he makes his way back to the group. He doesn't walk, he saunters. Hips swaying with each step, hands tucked in the pockets of his ripped jeans, Marcus strolls to his—our—friends like a model on a runway. When he gets to them he swings an arm over Romeo's shoulder and winks at me. When I don't respond he raises an eyebrow and dips his head towards Romeo's.

"Hun? Are you buying the lipstick or not?" The cashier's bored expression when I snap my head back to her reminds me why I'm here.

"Yeah. I mean, yes please." I correct, wincing at my rudeness. "Thank you," I make sure to say when she hands me my card and the bag a moment later. That's better.

Laughter drifts towards me as I make my way over to my friends. "…all over her face!" Rosie is laughing when I approach, bag in hand. "Are you hungry, Jules?"

I'm not, but I can tell from the wide eyes that Romeo and Benny are throwing my way that they are. "I could eat." The boys cheer at my words and quick-march out into the mall. "Wait, where are we going?" I jog to catch up. Marcus and Benny have Rosie by the elbows and are halfway down the fluorescent-lit corridor already.

"Wild Will's." Romeo is trailing after them but I don't follow.

"I'm sorry, where? I thought we were getting something to eat?"

Romeo waits for me to catch up, smiling that butterfly-inducing smile. I don't want my stomach to do that, this is *Romeo* for crying out loud, the biggest flirt I've ever known. I'm not here to date, I'm here to be a normal teenager. To have a normal teenage summer.

"It's the arcade that just opened at the end of the mall. They have food too. Come on, it's fun—I promise." He holds out a hand

and I take it, letting myself enjoy the shiver that runs through me at his touch, before I remind myself it doesn't mean anything. I'm not flirting, he's not flirting, it's just holding hands. Totally normal friend stuff.

We catch up to the others at the arcade entrance, Romeo dropping my hand when Rosie looks pointedly at him. Curious what a real arcade is like, I follow everyone inside the dark space. Rows of games stretch out, sets of them at different angles to separate the types. Bells ring and lights flash as we walk in, the electronic sounds overwhelming.

Snippets of songs and speeches assault me as we walk past. Some are dark, covered with bloody zombies or gory monsters. I lean into Romeo as we walk past those ones, as if they might leap out from the screen and snatch me away. We weave through crowds of people as Marcus and Benny debate the merits of one game over another. Other sections are sickeningly sweet with pastel cartoons and high-pitched singing. The noise they make is helped along by the dozens of younger kids clustered around them.

"See anything you want to try?" Romeo has to lean in close so I can hear him over the noise. "We could play a racing game?" He points to a row of motorcycles perched in front of their respective screens, the video in front depicting someone racing through the desert. I ignore the way my heart is racing and shake my head.

"Is there something less, video-y?" I have to pull his shoulder down so I can reach his ear and be heard. Is being close like this affecting him the same way it's affecting me? If it is, he's a better actor than I am. My voice sounds breathless and silly to my ears.

From down here, I study the sharp line of his jaw when an intense need to touch it hits me. My hand is halfway up before

I come to my senses and fiddle with my hair instead. What the heck is wrong with me?

"How about that one?" Romeo points to a bank of wooden lanes against the far wall. "Monkey, B-boy! Skee ball!" He shouts to the others through the crowd, before hauling me by the elbow towards the game. They catch up as Romeo finishes explaining how to bowl the balls up the ramp, aiming for the concentric rings to get points. A dim memory of doing this before with my dad surfaces, along with the realization that all those hours spent playing bocce ball with my mom are about to come in handy.

"Who knew the fairy princess was a ringer?" Marcus crows a few minutes later when my high score beats everyone else's. Laughing, I curtsey while the gang's compliments and complaints wash over me. Rosie gives me a thumbs up while Benny and Romeo complain. Marcus spins me under his arm, tucking me into his side for a second.

Maybe Romeo holding my hand isn't so special after all, if Marcus is doing the exact same thing. These guys are touchy feely in a way I'm not used to. Although, my stomach doesn't flip and my heart doesn't race when Marcus takes my hand to pull me towards an air hockey table. We play a couple of rounds, me and Rosie against Marcus and Romeo, then Marcus and Benny play against Romeo and Rosie.

The five of us hop from game to game, playing whatever strikes our fancy and snacking on soft pretzels. I still like skee ball best and convince them to play with me twice more, losing to Benny the second time, but winning the third. We tease each other and cheer for each other as we play, Rosie and the boys obviously easy in their friendship.

This is what I wanted when I came to visit. Normal. Fun. Friends.

Does it matter that every time I catch Romeo watching me my heart races? Or that Benny doesn't touch me or Rosie the way Marcus and Romeo do? Or that Marcus doesn't give me goosebumps the same way Romeo does?

We're slowing down on the games, wandering the space more than playing when I spy a photo booth in the back corner. "Can we?" I point at the booth, praying I'm not asking for something they all think is dorky.

"You want a photo to remember our handsome faces? Your wish is our command, Angel," Romeo answers before anyone else can argue. Rosie rolls her eyes but leads the way.

"Are we all going to fit?" I peer inside the space when we get there. The tiny bench looks big enough to hold maybe two or three people.

Marcus and Benny slide past me, sitting on the bench. "We'll make it work. Come on Rome, quit flirting and sit." Benny pats the sliver of bench space next to him. Romeo shoves Benny into Marcus and wedges himself inside. I have to laugh at the three of them—Marcus and Romeo shoved into the corners with Benny in the middle, half sitting on each of them in order to fit.

Marcus pats his legs. "Okay girls, who's sitting on my lap?" He eyes me with a grin, sending heat racing up my cheeks. I've never sat on a boy's lap before.

"Come here," Romeo grabs my hand and pulls me to sit on him, wrapping his arms tight around my waist. Marcus laughs, but Rosie eyes us and I shrink against him. Can he feel how fast my heart is beating? Can Rosie see what he makes me feel? Is it that obvious?

I'm just another one of the dumb girls he flirts with, aren't I? Stupid stomach, quit filling with butterflies every time he touches you. It doesn't mean anything. It's just Romeo being Romeo.

Rosie does something on the screen and then it counts down from five. "Smile!" Rosie calls and I'm blinded by the flash of the picture being taken. We make silly faces for the next two. Right as the fourth and final photo is snapped, Benny leaps up with a shout, knocking Rosie and I into Marcus and Romeo who tickle us both. I'm still laughing as we tumble out of the booth.

"Benny! You scared the crap out of me!" Rosie smacks him on the arm and he bows. "Now I have to pee. Don't abduct Jules, I'll be right back." Rosie walks off towards the bathroom.

"I'm getting a drink, you want one?" Marcus asks, already walking towards the snack bar on one end.

"Wait up." Benny quick steps to catch up. Neither of them look to see if Romeo and I are following.

I hesitate, not sure where to go. Romeo watches everyone walk away from us for a second before turning to me. "Come on." Mischief written all over that handsome face, he pulls me back into the photo booth. I sit on the edge of the bench while he fiddles with the screen.

"Do you trust me, Angel?" He turns around.

I swallow at the intense expression on his face. He's actually serious. "Why?"

"It was a yes or no question. Do you trust me?"

I study his face, silent. Those green eyes bore into mine, his jaw set. There's no hint of uncertainty in his face, unlike the million questions bubbling under my skin. But I do trust him. He's been my friend for years, even if all the butterflies and tingles he's sending through me now are brand new. It's Romeo. My

Romeo. Heart-stopping smile or not, I know the person behind the theatrics. I've seen the side of him he hides from everyone else. I trust the Romeo *I* know, the one in my letters.

"Yes."

"Good, because we almost ended up with a picture of my ass." He scoops me up off the bench and sits me on his lap again. But instead of wrapping his arms around me from behind, he turns me so we're facing each other, staring into each other's eyes. I hold my breath, the moment stretching out with sudden expectation. A light flashes while we sit there, staring at each other.

In slow motion, Romeo pinches my chin with one hand, tugging me close. Oh my gosh, what is happening? Like at the party, his lips brush against mine. His breath mingles with mine and I melt at the romanticness of it, even while every nerve in my body wakes up screaming for him to do something, anything—devour me, let me devour him. I can't describe it, but it's *everything*. My eyes flutter closed and all I can do is feel the moment, waiting for Romeo to kiss me properly.

I've read about a thousand first kisses, and nothing prepared me for how overwhelming it would be. My world narrows down to the sensation of his lips feather-light against mine, his fingers pinching my chin, his chest warm against my side and his thighs hard beneath me. It's been seconds and years while I wait. Just like my life, always waiting, almost living but never quite making it happen. I'm tired of waiting.

A flash goes off as I grip his shirt and pull him close. Startled at exactly the wrong time, instead of pulling him in for the kiss I imagined, our teeth smash and pain rockets through me. I gasp and Romeo jerks back, knocking me off his lap and onto the floor.

"Ow!" I don't know if I should rub my face or my butt, they both hurt.

"Jesus, are you okay, Juliet?" Romeo's working his lips and scrunching his face in pain. He reaches out a hand to pull me to my feet, but my long skirt gets in the way, I keep stepping on the edge while I'm getting my feet underneath me. Growling in frustration, I hike the fabric out of the way so I can get up like a human and not a newborn giraffe, both of us muttering apologies non-stop.

Romeo leans down and scoops me up, one arm sliding behind my knees, sending electricity through me at the sensation. Always covered by long skirts and dresses, so much of my skin is virgin, every touch is amplified by the newness of contact. On instinct, I wrap my arms around Romeo's neck just as another flash goes off. I completely forgot about the photos being taken.

"Can I have a do-over?" Romeo whispers, sitting back down on the bench. I'm still on his lap, cradled in his arms. At my nod, a smile I've never seen spreads across his face. It's not a mischievous grin and it's not the "you know you love me" smirk he flashes when he's playing the flirt. It's not even the genuine smile he's been sharing with his friends all afternoon.

No, this is a "Juliet, you just unlocked a hidden treasure" kind of smile. It's soft and secret, and I *know* deep in my soul that no one has ever seen it before.

Being brave, I cup his cheek with one hand. Partly because I don't know if I can resist touching him for a second longer, and partly to make sure this kiss doesn't end in disaster. Romeo keeps his hands where they are, one draped over my thighs, the other flat against my back, holding me in place. I lean in, and press my lips to his.

It's a safe kiss. No fireworks going off, but no teeth clashing either, just his lips against my lips and my heart thudding in my chest.

It's not enough.

Romeo must feel the same because he pulls back, takes a breath, and then his hands are holding my cheeks, his fingers cupping my neck and jaw, his kiss burning me up from the inside. Fire races up my spine, and I press into his arms, pulling him close. One last flash goes off as everything in me builds to an excruciating high. I don't know if I'm going to pass out from lack of oxygen, shout with joy, or cry.

But that kiss?

That kiss was *everything*.

CHAPTER ELEVEN

Romeo

I HAVE BEEN wrong about everything my entire life. I thought I knew what love was, what a kiss was supposed to be. I've kissed girls before. I've kissed a lot of girls. Some of them have been good kisses, some have been terrible.

But kissing Juliet?

This is kissing. This is more than just her lips touching my lips. This is my soul leaving my body and finding a home in her. I'll never belong to myself again. I've given myself—body, soul, heart—every molecule in my being is hers.

Her lips are soft and pliable beneath mine, the skin of her cheeks under my fingertips smooth and silky. I sneak a peek mid-kiss and am left even more breathless by the delicate curve of her closed eyelids, the sweep of eyeliner across her lashes, the perfect arch of her eyebrow.

I could spend the rest of my life here, drinking her in, and be happy.

"You might want to keep these where no one can see them." Benny's words break the spell we're under. Juliet pulls back with a gasp, her fingers flying to her lips. Her blue eyes are wide as saucers. She freezes for a second like a bunny caught in the headlights, before springing up off my lap and straightening her skirt, not meeting my eyes.

Something moves in my peripheral vision. Benny's hand is sticking between the curtains, waving two narrow strips of paper, the photos we forgot we were taking. I snatch them from his hand, handing one to Juliet. The first one is us staring into each other's eyes. I can see the uncertainty in my expression but am shocked at the set of Juliet's chin, tipped up just a smidge, defiance written in the tilt of her head. The second photo is a blur of our heads and shoulders, the disaster of that kiss too fast for the camera to capture, we're just a smear of light and dark on the paper.

In the third photo, all you see is my torso cradling her in my arms, you can't see either of our faces, just the drape of Juliet's skirt, the creamy expanse of one of her calves against my fingers. The photo brings back the way her silky skin felt, the way her muscles moved beneath my fingers. Just the memory of holding her, touching her, has my heart stuttering and leaves me light-headed.

But that last photo. The last photo captured a moment I'll never forget, as long as I live. The moment my world shifted on its axis and Juliet became the center of it.

"Romeo…" Juliet's trembling word drags me away from my thoughts. "Um. What?" She stumbles over her words and it's so adorable I want to kiss her all over again. She tucks her hair behind her ear and tries again. "Um. So…that was…I don't even know. We should go, right?"

Benny sticks his head through the curtain. "Yes, you should definitely come out of there *right now*."

I reach to take Juliet's hand but she pulls away, stepping past me and out of the photo booth, tucking her strip of photos in her purse as she goes. I pull my wallet out of my pocket and tuck the strip inside before slipping it back in and stepping out of the booth.

The second the curtain drops behind me, I understand why Benny was insistent. Rosie is rounding the corner of a nearby game, Marcus beside her. She's laughing at something he said but narrows her eyes at me and Juliet standing close. Jules scoots away from me, putting Benny between us before I can object. Did she not feel what I felt? Does she not want to be seen with me?

"Hey Jules, we should go. Sunday dinner waits for no one." Rosie announces as she comes into earshot.

Oh right, the famous Caplan Sunday dinners. I haven't been allowed to join one for years, but I remember them vividly. Rosie's parents insist on a formal dinner every Sunday night and if you live under their roof, attendance is non-negotiable. "Are they back? I thought your parents were out of town?"

Rosie shakes her head. "They got home yesterday and leave again tonight. They're taking the red-eye so we have time to have dinner before they leave. Joy." The sarcasm lacing Rosie's words gets a laugh from Marcus, but no one else. "But they're gone for two weeks after tonight, thank God."

Juliet sneaks a small smile in my direction. I want more than anything to reach behind Benny's back and touch her. Do I dare? Rosie and Marcus are making a joke about the ragers Rosie's going to throw while her parents are gone, and Benny is busy on his phone, probably texting Nikki. I take my chance and reach behind him to slide one fingertip along the back of Juliet's arm. She covers her gasp with a laugh as my finger reaches the palm of her hand. I curl my finger around her pinky, she squeezes back for an instant before pulling away.

"Come on, we should go." Juliet pulls Rosie along with her, waving at us before she leaves. I ignore Benny and Marcus as I watch her leave, taking my heart with her.

"Yo. Romeo." A finger snapping in my face brings me back to Earth. "Dude. You know she's off limits, right?" Benny shakes his head at me. "She's a Caplan, dude. She's *The* Caplan. Your dad would send you away to military school for real if he found out."

Marcus freezes, looking me up and down. "If they found out what exactly?"

I don't answer, just cross my arms and look away, following the blonde heads of Rosie and Juliet as they disappear out the entrance to Willy's. Benny answers for me. "Juliet's his next victim."

"She's not my 'victim', Benny, Jesus fuck." Anger surges through me at his choice of words. "She's my friend, okay?"

"I saw the pictures, Romeo, that's not just a friend. *Rosie* is your friend. Juliet…" He shakes his head. "You tell me."

How do I tell them that my world was irrevocably changed the moment my lips touched hers? They'll never believe me, not after all these years of me fumbling over every pretty girl we've met. "It's just different, okay?" I manage, dumb as it sounds, it's all I can give them. "I'm not going to hurt her. And I'm not stupid, I know she's a Caplan and I'm a Montgomery."

CHAPTER TWELVE

Juliet

I HEARD THE words Rosie said, but I don't understand what she means. "I know his last name is Montgomery? So?"

Rosie grabs my arm before we get to the bottom of the stairs, turning me to face her. Her blue eyes are serious, her mouth pinched in exasperation. "Do you remember right after you guys left?"

My forehead wrinkles while I think. "Kind of? I'm not sure what you mean. It was a long time ago, Rosie."

"When you guys sold your house to the Montgomery's, there was some kind of drama. I don't know the details, but his parents were *pissed* at your parents over something."

"They were?" A vague memory of my parents complaining about the people who bought our house back when we first left the US nags at me, but I was too young to understand at the time and I'd forgotten about it. "But why does it matter now? It was almost ten years ago."

I take a few steps down before Rosie catches up. "There's a lot of history there, but it's not my place to tell you. Just…don't mention we saw them today. My parents don't ask about my friends and I don't tell, but if the subject of Romeo Montgomery comes up we'll both have to sit through a tirade about how he's a terrible influence, why his dad is a piece of scum lawyer, and his mom is a doped up waste of oxy." Rosie flips a piece of hair out of her eyes. "It's just easier if you don't mention him."

I knew he was a terrible flirt, but the idea of Romeo being a terrible influence clashes with the boy I know from our years of writing letters back and forth. This is the boy who swore me to secrecy when he paid to replace his teammate's uniform when it got run over by the lawnmower after a practical joke gone wrong. He worries about Monkey—Marcus I guess—getting hurt by picking a fight with the wrong person one day. My friend that *I* worried about when he threatened to steal his mom's pills after a particularly bad week.

It's been a while since one of his letters worried me like that, but he's not a bad person. He's just got a lot of personality.

Rosie is still gripping my arm. I look down at her hand and sigh, defeat and worry bubbling in my stomach. "Sure, yeah, I won't say anything. I promise."

Aunty Cathy and Uncle Chuck are already in the dining room when I follow Rosie through the door. "Juliet, sweetheart, come here." Aunt Cathy hurries over, draping an arm over my shoulder and pulling me into the room. "I want you to meet Principal St. Clair." She leads me over to a tall, middle-aged man with a receding hairline not at all hidden by the few strands of dark hair combed over the top. He peers over the edge of his wire-rimmed glasses, assessing me. I try not to stare at the button straining to stay shut over his belly.

"Hello, young lady." Principal St. Clair's voice is surprisingly deep. "I hear there's a chance you may be joining us at Oak Hills Prep next year."

Shocked, I turn to Aunt Cathy. "Did you hear something from my parents?"

My mom sends me an email almost every day but hasn't mentioned anything new about me staying. As far as I know, it's still a question of the political unrest there settling down.

Aunt Cathy laughs. "Oh no dear, I was just mentioning to Principal St. Clair that it's been discussed, but nothing is decided. We were just discussing the logistics of placing you in classes, since your mom has been homeschooling you for all these years."

I hate the way people say 'homeschooling'. Like my mom had me in a cult or something. It's not like we had much choice—when you move constantly and live in a foreign country, it makes sense. Maybe my parents are a tad overprotective. It's possible I'm a little more sheltered than I thought, but so what? Just because I haven't been exposed to all the horrible things of the world doesn't make me a freak.

I smile instead of rolling my eyes like I want. "My mom can send you all the information you need. I already took my SAT's and a couple of AP tests last year. *If* I end up staying, I'm sure it will be just fine."

It better be more than fine. School, reading and dreaming about traveling are all I've done my whole life, it's about time it paid off.

"Watch out, Dad. This one is feisty." The familiar voice sends my stomach plummeting. "Nice to see you again Juliet."

I hide my grimace. "Uh, hi Perry." The smile plastered on my face is one I've practiced at countless dinners with my parents and whoever they'd invited over that evening. The one that says 'I'm just a sweet girl, nothing interesting to see here'. Being boring is safer than trying to hide. If you hide, people want to find you. If you're boring, people lose interest. That's exactly what I want. For Perry to decide I'm boring, bland, nothing worth noticing. "How are you?"

"You've met Juliet, son?" Principal St. Clair looks over my head as Perry comes to stand beside him. Now that they're together, I can see the resemblance in their brown eyes and the shape of their jaws. Perry's hair isn't as dark as his dad's and is tamed into another perfect swoosh across his forehead. They share the same calculating expression as they eye me, although I'm sure for different reasons. I shiver under their gaze.

"We met the other day. Unfortunately, it was just a brief meeting. I'm hoping to get to know you better soon, Juliet."

Is this guy for real? The Perry I met the other night was so easily offended it was laughable. The fake posh mannerism? The condescending tone? I'd rather eat rotten eggs than get to know him better.

I'm about to walk away and find Rosie when Aunt Cathy speaks. "Juliet dear, I've seated you and Perry next to each other tonight. I promised your father I would introduce you to some nice young men while you were visiting." Aunt Cathy's sugar sweet tone clashes with the way she's holding my arm tight, preventing my escape.

I make painful small-talk with Perry and his dad for a few more minutes until we find our seats. True to her word, my name is handwritten on a card next to Perry's. I stifle a cringe when he pulls out my chair for me, grinding my teeth when he squeezes my shoulders like a child once I've sat down. I'm so busy unfolding my napkin and spreading it on my lap that I'm startled by Perry's voice whispering in my ear.

"I've forgiven you for your rudeness the other night, Tinkerbell. Marcus and Romeo would make a saint swear." I sit stock still in my chair, fuming at the patronizing nickname and Perry's attitude. He takes my silence for agreement and continues. "You and I make sense. My dad is well-connected, your dad is well-connected. I'm class president and pitcher for the varsity baseball team, you're prettier than all the other girls at school. We'd be perfect together. Just think about it."

An ache in my jaw from clenching my teeth reminds me to relax my face. Rosie sends me a questioning look from her side of the table but I give a tiny shake of my head. I can't murder this boy in front of so many witnesses, even if he's a pretentious prick.

Dinner is one long exercise in patience. I'm pretty sure Perry, Aunt Cathy, Uncle Chuck, and Principal St. Clair spend the entire time pitching the idea of Perry and I dating, trying to convince me it makes sense. Why?

Because he's handsome.

Because I'm pretty.

Because he speaks Spanish and I speak French, Italian and a smattering of Greek.

Because Perry is a shoo-in for an Ivy League college. Not that anyone has bothered to ask me what schools I'm applying to.

Because I've had all the best education by my own mother— conservative trophy wife extraordinaire.

Okay, they didn't *actually* say that one, but it was pretty heavily implied.

I've resorted to non-verbal answers, since no one is listening to me anyway, when Principal St. Clair says something under his breath to Uncle Chuck and they start laughing.

"What was that, dear?" Aunt Cathy asks, saving me the trouble.

Uncle Chuck puts down his wine glass and smirks. "I was just pointing out the irony that I saw one of Montgomery's ads on the back of a bus the other day, being chased by an ambulance. That bottom-feeder is usually the one chasing them." Uncle Chuck turns his smirk to me. "You stay away from that Montgomery boy Juliet. He's nothing but trouble. Right, Perry?"

Perry looks down his nose at me where I sit silent and fuming. "He's no better than the trash he was raised by, even if they *do* have money. He's a decent catcher, but I truly can't stand him and his entourage. They're so loud and obnoxious."

"But—" A swift kick to my shin under the table and a hard look from Rosie reminds me not to open my mouth about Romeo.

What's one more dinner of swallowing down my opinions? Unlike my literary hero, Anne, I *can* hold my tongue when needed. After an excruciating evening, Rosie and I are finally released from the clutches of the adults to disappear upstairs.

I follow Rosie into her room and flop on her bed while she changes into pajamas. "Are Sunday night dinners always so…" I search for the right word.

"Horrible? Boring? Never-ending?"

I laugh and roll over onto my back to stare at the blue sky and fluffy clouds painted on her ceiling.

"Yes. It's not quite as bad when it's just us, but if there are guests over…" Rosie shudders. "Yeah. I'm sorry. It's the price we pay for unlimited spending money, I guess."

"Are they always so awful about Romeo?" Asking about him is a bad idea, but I can't help myself. What could possibly be so bad?

Rosie turns her head to look at me. "Don't."

"Don't what?"

"Don't fall for him."

Too late.

"Why not?"

"He may not be the kind of trouble my parents think, but he's his own kind of trouble. I know he's fun, and romantic, and sweet, and makes you feel like you're the center of his universe." Rosie sighs before dropping onto her stomach next to me. "But he has his own issues and I don't want to see you dragged into his drama, okay?"

Annoyed, I don't answer, staring up at the painted ceiling. Is it because everyone sees me as an innocent baby, to be protected from the real world? Every time my innocence is revealed, a splinter of anger digs into my heart.

Am I really that clueless? Or is there something else, something that no one is telling me?

Changing the subject, I poke Rosie's cheek. "Why are they trying to set me up with Perry? I'm surprised they aren't trying to set *you* up with anybody."

Rosie laughs. "Oh, they've already tried. My mom and Perry's mom, before she left, wanted nothing more than for Perry and I to get together. To combine the St. Clair and Caplan assets, as my dad would say."

"Assets?"

"The St. Clair's own a lot of property in this town, mostly on the poorer side of town, and my dad owns all that commercial real estate. They wanted to create an empire, I guess." Rosie shrugs, pulling herself up to sit. I stay where I am, stretched out on her bed, my legs dangling over the side.

Rosie looks back, then hops off the bed to go close the door. "Jules, if I tell you something, do you promise to keep it a secret?"

I mime crossing my heart. "Of course."

Rosie bites her lip and stares out her window at the tree in her backyard. "My mom's spent years trying to hook me up with all of her friend's sons. You know how all us girls are supposed to dream of our wedding day?"

I snort. "Ugh, I hate that. Does anyone still really do that?"

Rosie laughs, some of the tension leaving her. "Right? No one I know gives a shit. Probably because most of us have either watched our parents get divorced or be miserable together." She grins and comes back to sit next to me on the bed. "My mom is obsessed enough for the both of us, but also…"

The easy smile on Rosie's face falls and her shoulders go tense. I reach out to pat her knee. "Hey, it's okay. Whatever it is, I got your back Rose. I can keep a secret, I swear."

She bites her lips, not meeting my eyes. "I'm never going to date the boys she wants me to because…I like girls."

Her confession fills the air in the room, heavy and thick. The way she's biting her lips and picking at the bedding beneath us fills me with compassion. No wonder she wanted Romeo distracted from her. How does he not know?

"Okay." My acceptance must take her by surprise because Rosie's eyes snap to mine, wide and confused.

"Okay? That's it?"

I squirm, trying to shrug from my prone position. "What else is there to say? Okay, you like girls. You're still you, still my cousin. It doesn't change anything between us, Rose."

To my utter surprise, Rosie bursts into tears. I scramble to sit up and hug her. We sit there on her bed for a minute, Rosie crying into my shoulder while I hold on. I don't know what to say so I don't say anything at all, just squeeze her as tight as she's squeezing me.

The weight of her parents' expectations must be heavy. Her older brother Tyson got out last year when he went across the country for college, leaving Rosie to bear the brunt of it alone. No wonder she was so excited to have me come stay with them.

"You won't tell my parents will you?" Rosie asks once her tears slow. "Yours too. You know they'll freak out."

"I swear." I grimace at the reminder. My dad in particular would freak out, probably demand I come home so Rosie wouldn't be a bad influence on me. Wait…"That's, um, that's not why they think Romeo and his friends are bad influences is it?"

My question gets a snort in response. "Uh, no. Definitely not. Romeo is as straight as an arrow and Benny's been in love with Nikki for years. Marcus flirts with everything and everyone, but I'm pretty sure he just likes to get a reaction more than anything." Rosie flops back on the bed, her hair poofing out into a halo around her. "I've never actually said it out loud before, you know? That was kind of anti-climatic if I'm being honest."

That gets a laugh from me and I poke her side. "Sorry for not creating a bigger scene. Do you want a do-over?" My words remind me of Romeo's from earlier today and a blush heats the back of my neck. I cover it up by clutching my chest and pulling a face. "Oh! Rosie! What will we do? Your parents? What will they say? How can they ever accept this? That you'll never bring home a strapping young man for your dad to pretend to hate and your mother to swoon over? How can I ever bear to be seen with you? What if you…" I fake a huge gasp, covering my mouth with my hands. "What if you want to walk around holding hands, *in public,* with a girl?"

Rosie throws a pillow at me and laughs when I can't contain my giggles any more. "You suck! I honestly really wasn't sure how you would react, Jules. You know what our parents are like, and it's not like you were living in places known for being socially progressive."

She has a point, but… "There is such a thing as the internet in those places, Rose. And, yes, I read a lot of old books. But I also just read a lot. New stuff too." I put a finger to my lips. "That's the beauty of ebooks, no one sees the cover of what I'm reading." My parents don't know that I created my own Amazon account years ago so they wouldn't see what books I was buying.

Rosie's mouth drops open, no words coming out for a second. I smirk, but inside I'm shaking. I've never confessed to reading some of the books I do, authors like Emma Scott and books like *The Hate U Give* have taught me a lot about what kind of person I want to be, what kind of life I want to live.

But this conversation isn't about me.

"Rosie, I mean it. I won't tell anyone, not unless you want me to. But now I get why you wouldn't want them to force Perry on you. And why you wanted to distract Romeo rather than tell him. Although, I think he'd keep your secret if you asked him to."

Rosie shakes her head. "Romeo has his own problems, he doesn't need to add mine."

CHAPTER THIRTEEN

Romeo

MOM GIGGLES at the same time as Julia Roberts, missing the popcorn I toss at her, again. We're on the couch in the den, watching *Pretty Woman* for the fiftieth time, but even though I kind of hate this movie, I hate turning Mom down when she's in a good mood even more.

Besides, being here in the den gives me an excellent view of the lights and activity going on next door. Their formal dining room looks out over the backyard, I can see it if I angle myself just right.

"If your dad looked like Richard Gere, I'd wear whatever—"

"Gross, Mom. Stop." I interrupt her before she can finish that thought. "No way do I want to think about you and Dad and the same context as...that." I wave a hand towards the screen, then shove another fistful of popcorn in my mouth.

Mom grins, her head resting on the back of the couch. In the dim light I can pretend her glassy eyes are only reflecting the TV screen. That her dilated pupils are only from the dark. "One day you'll understand." She sighs. "It doesn't matter anyway. It's not like your Dad is ever home to sleep with me anyway."

"Mom!" I throw a few pieces of popcorn at her to make her stop. That is disgusting. I do *not* want to think about my parents doing anything close to, well, that. "Jesus Christ, Mom. Try not to traumatize me any more than necessary." Shuddering at the idea, I distract myself by sneaking another glance at the Caplan's house.

The window on the next wall has a great view of their front door, a fact I've taken advantage of countless times over the years. I would watch for Rosie's parents to leave before sneaking over to play video games with Tyson and eat whatever food Rosie could sneak out of the kitchen for me. I shift on the couch to get a better view.

"Pay attention. You know this is my favorite part." Mom's hand slaps my thigh.

"Sorry, sorry." I'm not, but it's not worth the fight.

All I need is to see Perry and his dad leaving after dinner, then I'll be able to sleep. Irritation at the thought of him being there with my Angel, Rosie too, has been gnawing at me ever since I got home and spotted them walking up the driveway. Rosie's complained over the years about how her mom and Perry's mom always tried to hook them up.

I may be a flirt, but I pursue girls because I *like* them, not because I think their parents are influential or because they would make me look good on a college application. Benny nearly murdered Perry when he overheard him telling Principal St. Clair that he was going after Nikki "because he could pass dating a scholarship student off as community service."

The light flicks on in Rosie's room, but not the one next door that used to be Tyson's, where Juliet is staying. I don't think they've realized that I can see straight into Juliet's room from mine. Tyson used to signal to me when it was safe to come over by flashing the light on his desk. I miss him, he was like the big brother I never had.

My phone lights up, earning me an irritated growl from Mom. I glance down to see it's from Benny.

> **BENNY:** Don't get mad, okay?
> **ME:** Why would I get mad?

I tap out the letters one at a time, careful to keep Mom from noticing. It's the shopping scene on Rodeo Drive, I've got a few minutes while that has her distracted. I grin to myself in the dark. Makeover montages may be Mom's favorite pastime, but teasing Benny is mine.

> **ME:** I'm not gonna get mad.
> **BENNY:** That's what you said last time…
> **ME:** I already apologized for that.
> **BENNY:** …

He sends me a gif of Zendaya rolling her eyes, surprising a snort from me. I sneak a glance at Mom and the TV, making sure she didn't hear. The saleswomen are still being snotty, I have time.

> **ME:** Okay, fine. I promise not to get mad.
> **BENNY:** Don't do it.
> **ME:** Don't do what?

A flash of light from next door distracts me from teasing Benny, as fun as it is. The garage next door opens and Chuck's

Lexus backs out of the garage and down the driveway. I keep an eye on it as the boring silver vehicle turns onto the main road and drives away. I must have missed the St. Clair's leaving.

I check on Mom before responding to the text that just buzzed in. The song accompanying the shopping montage winds down, alerting me that I better pay attention again.

"...mistake." Mom says with Julia Roberts, popcorn bits landing on her chest.

> **BENNY:** You know what I mean. It's a bad idea Rome, her aunt and uncle hate you. Your dad hates her parents. They'll never let you near her if they find out. It's only going to end with you being shipped off to military school or her being sent back to who knows where. Or both.

I don't deserve a friend like Benny. I shouldn't tease him, but I just can't help myself. Pretending to be obtuse is so much easier than admitting he's right.

> **ME:** I'm touched B-Boy. You really do love me!
> **BENNY:** I'm being serious. It's a bad idea. For fuck's sake, you're Romeo and Juliet, you should be running far away from her fast as you can. I don't believe in fate, but that can't be a good thing.

Without warning, pain shoots through my head, jerking me away from my phone. "Pay attention!" Mom's screech as she twists my ear hurts as much as her fingers pinching the cartilage. "Can't we just enjoy one fucking night? Or are your friends more interesting than me, huh?"

Shit.

"Mom, no. I'm sorry."

"Am I that boring to be with? First your father doesn't want anything to do with me, and now you? It's me, isn't it?" The screeching turns to tears. She's off the couch and halfway to her room before I can react.

Dammit.

With a huff, I flop back against the cushions. I give up. There's no point in chasing after her. She'll either cry until Dad gets home, and then he'll yell at me for making her cry, or she'll yell at me herself until she passes out on the bed and he'll find some other reason to yell at me.

In the dark, I creep to my room, avoiding the creaky spot by the bathroom to be safe.

Perching in my window, I stare at the house next door. Benny's right. I should be running. And not just because of our names. Our parents hate each other. They'll never see past what happened when we were kids. I should walk away.

But then the light flips on in Juliet's room and I'm treated to the sight that reminds me why I don't want to care about all that. I can't look away as she walks in and sits down on her bed. She pulls both legs up on the bed, hugging them close and resting her cheek on her knees, her face turned towards me. If I didn't know better, I'd think she was looking right at me, but there's no way she knows I'm here.

Do I turn on my own light so she knows?

Before I can make up my mind, she slips off the bed and rummages in her purse. Pulling out her phone and a piece of paper, it takes me a second to realize it must be her copy of the photos we took today. She studies the pictures as she walks back to her bed. I want to pull mine out of my wallet, but to see them I'd have to turn on the light and I'm not ready yet.

Not ready to know if I've been rejected or not.

I'm not stupid, I know that Perry and his dad were probably at their house for dinner to butter Juliet up. I saw the look on Perry's face when he stormed away on Friday night. He wasn't giving up—he was making a tactical retreat so he could regroup and try again.

Glancing across to her window, Juliet's taking something out of her closet. Are those pajamas? I flip my light on my desk, knocking over my pen holder, spilling them everywhere. Across from me, Juliet freezes in her room, eyes glued to my window, clutching the clothes in her hand to her chest.

I wave, like a dork, and mouth "sorry" across to her. She shakes her head. I hold up my phone and shake it. She shakes her head, then shrugs. Dammit, I don't have her number and she doesn't have mine. I don't want her to get it from Rosie either.

I hold up a hand, then start searching for the dry erase marker I know is somewhere on my desk. Spotting it tucked against my keyboard, I turn back to find her watching me, head cocked. I start to write my phone number on my window but halfway through realize that she won't be able to read it.

Too impatient to find a tissue, I whip my shirt off and use it to wipe the writing off and start over, this time carefully writing each number backwards from right to left. She squints across the way before smiling and pulling her phone out of her hand.

UNKNOWN: You just HAD to take your shirt off didn't you?

Grinning, I save her number before answering.

ME: I was impatient. How was dinner?

ANGEL: I can't answer that until you put your shirt back on.

ME: Too distracting for you? Or am I making you
hungry again?

Looking up from my phone, I catch her snort and the look of disgust she sends my way. I point finger guns at her and give an over the top wink. When she giggles, I start posing like a body-builder in the window. I wish I could hear it, but knowing I'm the one making her laugh has a goofy grin stretching across my face.

My phone buzzes against the desk. Assuming it's from Juliet I snatch it up, but the message on it is like a bucket of cold water dumped over my head.

DAD: On my way home. Did you clean up the backyard
like I told you to? What excuse am I getting this time? Dog
ate your brain? You better hope it's done.

I hate him sometimes.
And I fucking did it this morning, so the asshole can back off.
Another text pops up.

MARCUS: So are you flirting with Rosie or Juliet now? Just
want to make sure I keep it straight. 'Cause if you're not
going to flirt with Juliet (which would be the smart thing to
do) can I have a go?

All the smugness drains from me.

ME: Flirt with her and I'll kill you.

MARCUS: Which her?

ME: Touch Juliet and I'll snap your fingers. We can find a new outfielder.

MARCUS: Easy Tiger, I was just kidding. Don't do anything stupid.

Throwing my phone down on my bed, ignoring the buzz of incoming messages, I look up to find Juliet staring at me through the window. God, she must think I'm insane. A second ago I was goofing off for her and now I'm a moody bastard throwing my phone. Everyone is right, she'd be better off without me.

Her light flashes, catching my attention. She's holding up her phone and wiggling it, her other hand pointing at the bed. I turn to look and see her name flashing on the screen.

"Hey."

"Hey, are you okay? You look like something upset you." Her voice in my ear while I can see her standing in her room is torture. So close, but so far away.

"I'm fine. It was just Marcus being an a-hole." I leave out Dad's message. The longer I can hide my dysfunctional family from her, the better.

"Oh. That's okay. I thought maybe I did something." She sounds so unsure.

"No Angel, it wasn't you at all. I promise. Are you okay? I saw Perry and Principal Prick leaving. Did he give you a hard time about the other night?" I go to perch in my window again and she does the same, tucking her legs underneath her long skirt. I don't take my eyes off her as we chat. I drink in her expressions, the way she fidgets with the fabric, traces shapes on the glass.

"It was fine, I guess. Principal *St. Clair...*" She emphasizes his name and I grin. "…was letting me know that he thinks they can figure out what classes I'd be in if I end up staying in the fall."

"Do you want to stay?" Please stay, please want to stay here and not go back to Europe. "In your last letter, you said you wanted to know what normal high school was like."

She traces a heart on the glass. "I did, didn't I? I don't know Romeo. I want to stay…but even as strict as they are, I miss my parents. But, if they were here…" She trails off, leaving the words unspoken, but I'm pretty sure I can guess what she's thinking. "I don't know what I want, truthfully."

"If they were here, there is no way we could see each other, right? And I really want to see you more." The words are out before I stop to think. it's true, I just want to be near her all the time. "Let me take you on a real date."

She looks up, straight into my eyes, even from so far away. "This is crazy, right? I met you two days ago. Things shouldn't be this…intense? It's too fast. Isn't it?"

I don't answer right away. I can't. Juliet's taken my breath away with her words. She feels it too, this overwhelming need to be together. "We didn't meet two days ago. I've known you for five years." I lean back against the window frame, tapping the window with my finger. "I know your favorite color is purple. Your favorite book is actually *Anne of the Island*, not *Anne of Green Gables* like you tell everyone. I know that you don't like chocolate or sour candy, but can't resist a cupcake. The only difference is that now I don't have to wait two weeks to hear your answer to my questions or to get your terrible advice."

That gets me the laugh I was hoping for. I grin at the outrage on her face and laugh out loud when she sticks her tongue out at me through the window.

"I do not give terrible advice!"

"Do you see a girlfriend anywhere, Angel?" I make a show of looking around my room. "If your advice is so good, what would you tell me to do to win over the current object of my affections?"

Her face falls and her body slumps against the wall at her back. "I'd tell you to change your name. Why do you have to be a Montgomery? Why can't you be anything else? You'd still be you, right?"

"A rose by any other name would smell as sweet." I joke, but the words are true. Juliet's sigh in my ear echoes my own. "I don't know about you, but I would prefer to avoid the tragedy we seem to be destined to."

Juliet's laugh is tired. "Yeah. It's so stupid. Star-crossed and all that."

"You can't say it can you?"

"Say what?"

"Lovers."

She ducks her head, hiding her face from me and I know I've struck a nerve. "I can too," she whispers into the phone without turning back to look at me.

"Jules, I—" But I'm interrupted by the flash of headlights turning into my driveway. "Shi—shoot. My dad's home. I gotta go. Talk to you tomorrow?"

"Don't forget to put your shirt on. Goodnight Romeo."

"Goodnight, Juliet."

I hang up and toss my phone on the bed before going downstairs to face my dad's inevitable disappointment.

CHAPTER FOURTEEN

Eleventh Grade

ROMEO,

In your English class have you had to read that story about the woman with the yellow walls who's slowly going crazy? As you can see from the return address, we finally got to move into the new house. And guess what?

One of the bedrooms has bright pink wallpaper. Like, Pepto Bismol pink.

And guess who gets that room? That's right, me. I hate it. I hate it so much, but we're not allowed to take it down and my mom insists it's "perfect for me." Because I guess in my mom's eyes I'm still ten years old, not almost sixteen. It's so ugly I can't even imagine it away.

But I have a plan. I'm going to save up my allowance and get some plain sheets to hang over it so I don't go crazy staring at the pink walls. Maybe I'll even paint the sheets. I'm not sure, I haven't decided yet.

Why are you asking about grand gestures? Who's it for?

What about a picnic? I've always wanted someone to take me out for a picnic. Of course, I can never decide if I want a lunchtime picnic in a grassy meadow with a chance to swim in a swimming hole, or if I want to go on a nighttime picnic and stargaze afterwards. Which do you think is better? You know what no one ever talks about in books or tv shows when they go on picnics? They never talk about the bugs. There has to be bugs, right?

You know what you could do? Make her a bouquet of all her favorite snacks and candy! Of course, you'd have to find out what they are…do you know this girl well enough to guess? I noticed you never mentioned a name, afraid I'm going to add her to the list?

Wait…it's someone who's already on the list, isn't it? Romeo, it better not be Melody. Melody was bad news—don't you remember how she dumped all your baseball gear out the window when you were driving and got in a fight? Don't do it! Besides, isn't she friends with Sarah Dempsey? You *just* broke up with Sarah, again. Dating her friend again right afterwards is pretty sketchy. I don't know if we can be friends if you're going to do that.

Ignore that, I didn't mean it. The heart is a fickle thing, it wants what it wants. If you're in love, what can you do?

I've come to the conclusion that my heart is entirely practical. I've had chances to fall in love and I never have. I realize that my options out here are limited, but there was a really cute boy who lived on our street back in Istanbul, I *could* have had a crush on him, if I wanted to.

Slowly losing my mind in Sicily

JULES,

You can't be serious! You *could* have had a crush on him? That's not how love works. You either feel it or you don't. I should know, I've felt it enough times.

Maybe I'm just making up for all the opportunities you're not taking. Maybe *you're* the reason I'm so unlucky in love. The universe is using us to balance each other out—I'm always falling in love and you never are.

If that's true, I think the universe owes us each an apology.

And I'm not just saying that because it *was* Melody and you were right. I took her on a picnic, like you suggested. It was lunchtime and I just happened to know where there's a swimming hole. I had it all planned out—I packed sandwiches and soda, I even got the good chips, the kettle-cooked kind. I figured if I was lucky we could go skinny-dipping in the river afterwards.

I'm telling you Jules, I don't know what horrific crime I must have committed in a past life, but it had to have been bad. We were having a nice time—Melody only complained a little about the peanut butter and jelly—when a bee landed on her sandwich right before she took a bite. If you're thinking that she bit the bee and got stung on the tongue you would be right.

Not only did that ruin any chance I had of scoring an epic 'getting back together' make-out session, but it turns out that Melody is allergic to bees. I had to stab her with an EpiPen then take her to the ER. Not exactly how I wanted to touch her butt.

Anyways, enough about my failed date. How's the room redecoration going? Not planning to make the walls purple are you? I personally feel that purple walls would be just as bad as pink. If you really wanted to freak your parents out you could look for black or red sheets, then they'd think you were turning into a devil-worshipper. Ha! That would be hysterical.

Okay, it's probably funnier for me to imagine than it would be for you to live with. Parents are so unreasonable sometimes. My mom lost her shit the other day because she said I was being too loud. Too loud? I was in the den playing video games with Monkey and B-Boy, I didn't even know she was home. Of course, she didn't say anything until my dad was home so then he got mad too. Excuse me for being a normal kid and making a little noise. It's always better when I sneak over to Rosie's to hang out with her and Tyson. Monkey's house is the best though, his parents are never home so we can do whatever we want. It's too bad he lives kinda far, but once I get my license I can go over whenever I want.

Do you think your parents would ever let you come back here to visit?

ROMEO

CHAPTER FIFTEEN

Juliet

A KNOCK ON the door and a buzzing from my phone send me flying down the stairs. Rosie scrambles out of the kitchen and beats me to the door, flinging it open.

"Rome? Why are you here?" Her cocked hip takes up most of the doorway as she eyes my date. His dark jeans and short-sleeve button down, half tucked in, are more stylish than I've ever been. I wave at him over her shoulder and get a grin in response. Rosie turns her head to glare at me. "Jules…"

"I know what I'm doing, I promise. Would it make you feel better if you came with us?" I give her my best smile, praying that she turns me down.

After eyeing me for a second, Rosie sighs and moves aside. "I have a hair appointment." She snaps a hand out to grab Romeo by the shirt and glare at him. "Don't do anything stupid. If you hurt her, I'll murder you. And then I'll let our parents murder you all over again."

Romeo just grins at her, reaching an arm under hers to snag my hand. "I'll be on my best behavior. Promise!" he adds as he tugs me, giggling, through the doorway. We slow down as we cross over to his driveway, his Jeep parked on the street in front of his house. I laugh as he pulls on my hand, twirling me under his arm before stopping at the door of his car. He helps me climb inside, tucking my long dress under my leg so it doesn't flap, before climbing in himself.

"So, where are we going?"

Romeo doesn't do anything but grin at my question, turning his attention to pulling out into the street. I poke his thigh. "Where are we going?" I ask again.

"Trust me, you'll like it."

My arguments leave me at the knowing smile on his face. Instead of pestering him for an answer, I turn up the music, drowning out my questions with the wind whipping my hair in my face.

It's only when we pull up in front of an old-fashioned ice cream parlor that I get an inkling of what Romeo has planned. "Ready?" He grins at my delighted squeal.

I follow him inside, biting back my sighs at the perfect setting. The floor is tiled in black and white, white wrought-iron tables and chairs dot the floor, the seats upholstered in an adorable pink and white striped fabric.

But the crowning glory is the ice cream counter. Frost tickles the edges of the glass fronts, revealing an array of flavors. Behind the counter, a couple of teenagers serve customers while dressed in the red and white striped shirts and paper soda jerk hats of my dreams. One of the guys looks familiar, but I can't think of his name as we make our way to the front of the line.

"Hey Fitz." Romeo nods as we step up to the counter.

Fitz's curly red hair is pulled back in a bun at the nape of his neck—a stray curl pokes out from under his cap, bouncing wildly against his freckled cheek as he speaks. "Hey man, how's it going?" He jerks his chin at Romeo before studying me. "You're Rosie's cousin, right? Steph told me about you."

Romeo tugs me closer, shifting to wrap an arm around my waist, pulling me into his side. "Steph and Fitz have been together for ages."

My stomach flips at the contact, the warmth of Romeo's body contrasting with the cool air in the shop. "They started dating back when we were freshmen, right?"

Fitz nods at Romeo's question. "Yup. She's my girl."

I'm having a hard time picturing the friendly guy in front of me with the rude and judgemental girl I met at Rosie's house the other night. He must know something I don't. I lean into Romeo's side. "Maybe you should have been asking Fitz for advice all these years, instead of me. He's the one with a long-term girlfriend."

Romeo and Fitz burst out laughing at my statement. After a second, Romeo catches his breath enough to answer. "Yeah right. I'm pretty sure Steph just pointed at him in the cafeteria one day and said, 'We're dating now' and that was it."

It's easy to see Fitz's blush, his skin is so pale, and I sympathize. I can't hide it when I'm embarrassed either. I give him a smile and he shrugs. "What do you guys want?"

"Before you say strawberry," Romeo says, cutting me off and turning back to Fitz. "Can she try the raspberry cheesecake?"

Between Romeo and Fitz's suggestions I try half a dozen samples before settling on cherry vanilla. Romeo insists that Fitz turn it into a sundae, complete with whipped cream, sprinkles and another cherry on top. I'm in awe as Fitz expertly assembles my sundae and Romeo's triple chocolate fudge sundae, before handing them over to me while Romeo pays. I wander over to a table by the window.

The warm sun heats the glass to my side, while the blasting air conditioner raises goosebumps on my other arm. The contrast has my skin tingling and hyper-aware of every brush against it. Or maybe that's from being near Romeo. On a date.

I'm on a date with Romeo Montgomery.

Me.

Juliet Caplan.

For a girl who's never disobeyed her parents, I picked a heck of a way to start.

Romeo settles into the seat opposite me, pulling his sundae closer and handing me the spoon I forgot to grab. "Well, Angel, how am I doing so far?"

I take a bite of my ice cream before answering, the creamy, sweet taste of cherries filling my mouth. "Well, since it's my first real date, the only thing I can compare it to is my imagination." I wave my spoon in the air, then scoop up another bite of ice cream to stall for time and gather my thoughts.

He grins at me. "Well?"

"I think you're doing pretty good." The smile that lights up his face at my confession is sweeter than the ice cream on my tongue. "You know, everyone keeps telling me that I'm too innocent for you, that you're a bad influence, yada, yada, yada." I shrug. "I don't see it. What am I missing?"

I regret the words the moment I say them, because the sweet smile is gone from Romeo's face.

"Nevermind," I stumble over the word I say it so fast. "We don't have to talk about it." I reach across the table to squeeze

Romeo's hand. Again, electricity sparkles up my arm from the simple touch. I smile and he gives me a small smile in return.

"Jules..." He swallows and laces his fingers with mine. "I don't want to tell you, but I feel like I should. It's only fair that you know some of the things I've left out of my letters to you."

He looks away and lets go of my hand to spoon some of his ice cream in his mouth. I pull my hand back, his touch burned into my skin, and do the same. The cold of the ice cream settles in my veins. Or maybe that's worry from Romeo's tone.

"They all say I'm a bad influence because I've had some... issues...over the years." His face goes bright red and I reach across the table for his hand again but he keeps them in his lap, stubbornly looking away from me. "I'm not always fun to be around. I have good days and bad days. Your aunt and uncle probably think I'm just being dramatic, or that I'm doing it for attention. I just—I just need you to know it's not you, it's literally in my head. I don't always know when I'm having a bad day until I say something I regret."

The dejected look on his face, as if he's convinced I'm going to run away because of his words tugs at my heart. "Hey." My soft tone has him meeting my eyes again. "No one's perfect, right? I'll do my best not to take it personally. And if I think you're out of line, I'll tell you." I swallow. Confrontation is the thing I avoid at all costs. "Well, I'll try."

When Romeo doesn't say anything, I fill the silence by taking an enormous bite of my ice cream. I can't think of anything else to add. Is there more to this than he's saying? "Romeo? Was there something else?"

The smile drops back into place on his face like the sun peeking out from behind a storm cloud. If I hadn't seen his haunted expression earlier, I wouldn't have known it was there at all. "Nothing we have to talk about today."

Our afternoon is the storybook date of my dreams.

I push Romeo's confession to the back of my mind, determined not to let it ruin the day. I'll worry about it later.

We finish our sundaes before Romeo takes me to see a movie. During a few of the scarier moments, I hide my face in his chest until he wraps an arm around my shoulder and holds me close. Finishing the movie cuddled under his arm fills me with warmth and feeling of rightness.

After the movie, we take our time before going home. Whatever problems he's had in the past, the boy walking by my side has been nothing but a gentleman all night. Caring and considerate. We've talked about the books I've been reading, his hopes for next year's baseball season. I don't understand why anyone could think he was anything but great.

Sure, some of his letters in the past were a little dark. He wrote about his mom's pills, but I never thought it was serious. I assumed he was telling me things he was too scared to say out loud to anyone else. Doesn't everyone confess things to a penpal that you wouldn't say in real life?

I know I did.

Walking through the mall after the movie, electricity sparks in the air between us. It's been a perfect afternoon, but I can't stop thinking about my promise to call him out if his behavior confuses me. Can I really do it? Speaking up for myself is so hard. What if I hurt his feelings? What if hurting his feelings sends him into a bad mood and brings about the exact thing he warned me of? Now that it's daylight and we're in public, he's not touching me or holding my hand like I expected. Is it okay for me to ask him why?

There's no way he can get upset with me for asking a simple question, right? I steel my nerves and think through how I want to word it.

He's in the middle of telling me a story from one of his baseball games last year when I interrupt. "Romeo?"

"Yeah, Angel?" We stop walking, the smell of melted butter from the pretzel place a few doors down wafting into my nose. The strap of my purse keeps my hands occupied, while I sway on my feet, afraid to look him in the eye.

"This is a date, right?" The words burst from me, tinged with all the confusion I'm feeling. Regretting them immediately, I babble on. "Nevermind, that was a stupid question. I don't know why I asked. Just ignore me. It's fine, I'm fine, don't—"

I'm cut off by Romeo's lips, his kiss swallowing the river of questions I couldn't dam up inside me. One of his hands slides across my cheek to hold the back of my head, pulling me close. The other slips down my shoulder to pull my hand free of my purse strap, his fingers twining with mine.

I've read a lot of books. I've read a lot of kisses being described as tender, or demanding, or tongues slipping inside and everything in between. I've devoured stories about the world fading away, or electricity sparking between two people.

And that first kiss? The *real* one in the photo booth? Yeah, it had all of those things. I assumed it was first kiss magic or something. Like, only the first one got to be like that.

But this kiss is just as electric as the first. Again, my world fades to nothing except Romeo's lips on mine and his hand on the back of my neck. Every inch of me touching him is on fire, the rest longing to jump into the flames with it. Will it always be like this? Will I always hunger for him? Ignore the world, my parents, my good sense, when I'm with him? He is my drug. But not because he makes me forget the rest of the world. Romeo makes everything better, brighter, more alive just by being near.

"Jules, this is absolutely a date." Romeo says with a grin once he pulls away. "I just wasn't sure what you were comfortable with."

We walk again, hand in hand, passing people busy going about their days who don't care who we are or what our families think of it. "I…" I swallow down my nerves. "I want this to be a date. I want this." I squeeze his hand. "But, I know my parents would forbid it, yours would too."

Romeo holds the door open for me a step outside, the hot sun hitting me after the cool air inside. He takes my hand again and leads the way to his car. "Angel, I don't know what to do either. Of course, I want to shout from the rooftops that you're my girl. That I, the fu—screw-up Montgomery—have the most amazing girl in the world. And that by some trick of fate, I've convinced her to tolerate me." He puts a finger on my lips when I open my mouth to protest. "But I also know that the second I do, you'll be whisked behind a wall so high I'll never see you again. The question is, do we do the smart thing and keep our dating on the down low? Do we do the smart*er* thing and just stay friends?" We walk to the car in silence. I don't know what he's thinking, but I can't get past the thought that I don't know how I can be just friends with him. Not when every cell in my body aches for him.

He helps me climb into the passenger seat, tucking my dress back under my legs with a soft caress. Rounding the front, I'm fascinated by the way his biceps flex as he lifts himself into his seat. Romeo turns on the engine before turning to look at me.

"Or do we do the smart*est* thing and avoid each other all summer. Because honestly, I don't know if I can do anything besides want you so desperately it feels like I'm dying every time we say goodbye."

CHAPTER SIXTEEN

Romeo

THE FAINT sound of Billy Crystal and Meg Ryan's snarky banter drifts into the kitchen from the other room. I freeze, the plates in my hands halfway to the shelf. The heavy footsteps coming towards me aren't Mom's.

"You were supposed to do that last night." The irritation in Dad's voice is colored by early morning gravel.

I slide the plates onto the shelf and turn back to the dishwasher for the next item to put away. "I know, but it was late when I got home and then Mom—"

"Don't care about your excuse this time. I said it needed to be done yesterday. Trying to sneak it in before I get up in the morning doesn't count." He smacks the back of my head, hard, as he passes me on his way to the coffee maker.

"Ow. Jesus, Dad. I'm getting it done." My phone buzzes in my pocket. It has to be Jules, but I don't dare pull it out while Dad is here. He pulls a coffee pod out from the organized caddy beneath the machine while I pull the silverware basket out and take it over to the cutlery drawer.

I work in silence for a few seconds until something hits my back with enough force to sting. "What the hell?" Whirling, I kick something on the floor behind me.

"How many times have I told you to clean up after yourself?" Dad's voice is cold, but I can hear the anger simmering underneath. "Throw your goddamn trash away."

On the floor at my feet, is a used coffee pod. I only need to see its golden color to know it's not mine. "That's Mom's."

Dad pushes the button to start his coffee brewing before leveling me with a glare. "Don't blame shit on your mother. It's still warm." I could argue. Tell him I watched her make coffee *after* I made mine, but I bite my tongue instead.

Anger flares in my chest but I push it down. If I get into it with Dad this morning I'll ruin my chance to go out with Jules. The sputtering of the Nespresso machine on the counter is the only sound as we face off.

He leans against the counter, arms crossed and eyes narrowed. Dad's dark gray suit is perfectly pressed, the deep maroon of his shirt and solid black tie compliment his olive skin and dark hair. We have the same sharp jaw and cheekbones, even if I inherited my mom's full mouth. I hate that any part of me looks like him.

"She's in the other room. You can go see for yourself." I shouldn't send him after her, if they get into it I'll never get out of here on time to meet Jules, but I'll be damned if I take the blame for Mom. I need to finish unloading the dishwasher, but I refuse to step back into Dad's reach.

The last sputters and squirts of Dad's coffee echo in the silence between us. When the machine cuts off, the unmistakable sound of Meg Ryan's laugh drifts into the kitchen.

With a defeated sigh, Dad pinches the bridge of his nose. Without a word, he takes his travel mug and stalks into the other room. He's barely out of the room before I have my phone out to see what Jules said.

> **ANGEL:** They haven't left yet. What if they never leave? Should we make a different plan?
> **ANGEL:** Is everything okay?

I type out a response, ignoring the shouting from the other room.

> **ME:** It's fine. Just waiting for Dad to leave for work.
> **ME:** We don't have to change the plan, it'll work out. You'll just have to hike faster.
> **ANGEL:** Who says I'm the slow one?

I love it when my Angel is sassy in the morning.

> **ME:** Any idea what the hold up is on your end?

The problems on my end are currently yelling at each other over the sound of Mom's movie. Arguing with your partner in a rom-com is cute. In real life? Not so much.

I tune them out and focus on finishing up. Dad is trying to convince her to go to bed. I don't know why he bothers, she'll pass out eventually. I gave up trying to help her last summer. She's never going to change—he might as well accept it, like I have. Besides, watching old movies at three in the morning is a great way to distract yourself from the dark thoughts in your own head.

ANGEL: From what I can tell, his coffee wasn't right, so he's waiting for Cathy to make him a new one. And complaining about it very loudly. I don't know how Rosie is sleeping through this. Even if we weren't going out, I would have been woken up by the noise. I'm sure he broke something in the kitchen.

ME: Rosie sleeps like the dead. Also she's probably used to it.

ANGEL: True. I'm not used to the yelling. My dad never yells.

The garage door slams behind Dad as the volume on the TV doubles. I peek out the kitchen window to catch Dad's Porsche taking off down the street. Finally.

It's impossible for me to imagine what it must be like to have parents who never yell. My memories from before mom's accident, before everything fell apart, are hazy. I pace back and forth in the kitchen until I see Chuck drive away.

ME: Meet me at the car?

ANGEL: I'll be there in two mins.

"I don't like sneaking around. It feels wrong." Juliet starts talking the moment I come into view. She's already leaning against my Jeep, dressed for a day outside. Leggings hug her calves and thighs, her butt covered by a long tank top that I know she borrowed from Rosie. It's a new look from the usual long skirts and dresses and I like it. Her short blonde hair is tucked into a baseball cap, but it doesn't hide the worry in her eyes or the way she keeps pulling the back of her shirt down.

"Good morning to you too, Angel." I help her climb in before rounding the car and swinging myself inside. "It's our parents who are in the wrong and you know it. If they would get over themselves, we wouldn't have to sneak around." We've had this argument at least three times in the last four days. Juliet gets wrapped up in feeling guilty, until I remind her that we're the ones who are being open-minded and reasonable, not our guardians.

I don't hold mom's issues against the Caplans, why can't my dad let it go too?

My anger from being yelled at this morning stirs in my belly. I don't want to take that out on Jules, she doesn't deserve it, so I push it aside and flip a switch in my brain. It's time for Fun Romeo to take over.

Our day together is one of the best I can remember. The way Juliet appreciates the small beauty around us as we hike—a spiderweb sparkling in the sun, a tiny wildflower growing in the shade of a bush—and it pushes the dark thoughts in my head away. I could watch her watching a lizard on our path all day. How can the world be so bad when there's someone like Juliet in it?

We get home just in time, Juliet disappearing into the Caplan's house only moments before Cathy's Lexus rounds the corner. She scowls at me as she drives past. Well, I assume she's scowling at me, her face doesn't move much. I wave cheerfully, because as much as I want to be a better guy for Juliet, her aunt is a different story and I'm still an asshole at heart. My phone buzzes in my pocket as she pulls into the driveway.

ROSIE: Don't piss off my mom stupid. You're lucky she was late coming home.

ME: Are you spying on me Rosie? You missed your chance
with me, babe.
ROSIE: Pig.
ROSIE: I was keeping an eye out for Jules, you idiot.

A curtain at one of the upstairs windows flicks, revealing
Juliet and Rosie, grinning and waving down at me. I make sure
no one is looking before waving back and blowing a kiss to Jules.

ROSIE: Ugh. You two are disgusting. Go hang out with your
boys or something, she's mine for the rest of the night.

MASHING MY thumb down on the controller, I take my
shot and have the satisfaction of seeing Benny's player
drop, his half of the screen flashing a giant "game over"
graphic. "Boom! Take that!" I jump up, throwing my arms up
over my head, bowing and waving to my imaginary adoring
fans. Marcus helps me out by adding the roar and whoops of the
crowd. Benny adds some boos, for realism, before he tosses his
controller on the couch behind his head and flops to the side,
sprawling on the carpet in the den.

I sneak an unnecessary glance out of the window, but no
one has driven up in the last ten minutes. I would have heard
them if they had, my ears tuned to the frequency of Perry St.
Clair's stupid BMW.

"Dude, stop watching, they're not back yet." Marcus calls me
out cheerfully. "Let's go get burgers, I'm starving. Winner buys."

"I'm in. Eating is better than sitting here and waiting for the girls to come home." Benny rolls onto his back before doing a kip up to stand. "Maybe this is a good thing."

I glare at him as I check my pockets for the essentials. He's right, as usual, but I'm not going to pretend I'm in a good mood for these guys. "What's a good thing? Perry and Conner taking the girls out?" Watching helplessly through my window as Perry and Conner drove off with my girls brought on a dark cloud like I haven't felt all summer.

Not even Juliet's text, explaining that she and Rosie got ambushed by a double date set up by her aunt, could shine a light into my stormy thoughts. Her snarky updates on the awful movie he picked *should* be reassuring, but I can't bring myself to enjoy them.

Benny shrugs. "Both of your lives would be easier if you didn't actually date, you realize this, right?"

"I don't want to talk about it anymore. Can't you just be happy for me?"

Benny doesn't back down though. "I promise to let it go after this, but hear me out. It would be better for you both if you backed off. Let her date someone like Perry or Conner—someone her family approves of." I hate that Benny's right, that his words are reasonable.

I can't even be irritated at him, because I know he's just looking out for me, like always. Marcus and I would have been in way more trouble over the years if it hadn't been for Benny.

But the thought of Perry sitting next to Juliet in a dark movie theater right now has my blood boiling and my hands itching to punch him in the face. "If that douche St. Clair so much as touches her tonight, I will rip him apart." The words rumble out of my chest as we make our way out the front door and pile into Benny's car.

"I'll give you that," Marcus says, sliding into the front seat. "But you have to admit, Conner's a good guy. Hell, I don't know that I would make too much of a fuss if he dated Melody. Listen." He twists in the seat to look back at me as Benny pulls away from the curb. "I don't want to be reasonable either—it goes against my nature—but wouldn't it be easier for everyone if you guys just let it go and didn't try to re-enact the world's most famous tragedy?"

I bang my head against the seat rest behind me. I know they're right, but every cell in my body wants her. Just thinking about her choosing someone like Conner over me—because Marcus is right, he's a decent guy—feels like someone ripping my guts out and showing them to me while I'm still alive.

Okay, yes, I watched Braveheart with my mom last night. She was in a good mood, I guess 1990's Mel Gibson will do that, and I couldn't resist her invitation. The good days are few and far between. It probably helped that my dad is gone all week for a conference in Chicago.

"I *know* it would be easier. Juliet does too. But we can't help it, it's like, fate or something. We were just…meant to be. Tragedy and all."

Marcus and Benny share a look in the front seat, then Marcus shrugs. "It's your funeral, man. But if you two are really determined to be together, we've got your back."

CHAPTER SEVENTEEN

Juliet

I'M NOT sure who's going to snap first—me, Rosie, or Conner. Or possibly the waiter, who's been standing by our table for the last ten minutes while Perry mansplains the menu back to him. I make a mental note to leave an extra tip for the poor guy.

When Aunt Cathy told Rosie and me we were going out to dinner tonight and to go get dressed, this was not what either of us had been prepared for. Especially after last week's disaster, we both specifically told her that we weren't interested in her setting us up on any more dates. Romeo, Benny and Marcus had come stalking out his front door the second we pulled up, ready to snatch Rosie and me away. Only Rosie and I standing between them kept fists from flying as Perry gloated about taking us to a movie.

Assuming there was no way Aunt Cathy would have the gall to do that to us again, we'd giggled and shared the sink in Rosie's bathroom, putting on makeup and curling our hair. We assumed that at worst, we would have to spend an hour or so with Chuck and Cathy. The absolute horror that dawned in my mind and on Rosie's face as we came downstairs and discovered Perry St. Clair standing there talking with Uncle Chuck, was only eased a tiny bit by the sheepish look on Conner's face as he mouthed 'I'm sorry' at us.

"My father and I came here with Representative Beauchamp last summer. Rather disappointing service, but the beef is imported from Japan." Perry hasn't shut up about who he and his father know since he picked us up an hour ago. He may actually be worse than Draco Malfoy. If it wouldn't get me sent straight back to my parents, I'd have punched him in the nose already.

But then again, I'm not sure if Rosie or Conner wouldn't beat me to it. Conner, bless him and his all-American, boy next door charm, is trying to hide the way he rolls his eyes every time Perry name-drops another person we don't care about. The strain in Rosie's neck is all I need to see to know she's grinding her teeth so hard they're going to crack any minute.

"Perry?" I grit my own teeth as I lay my hand on his arm to interrupt. "Were you going to order anything else, or are you sharing with the rest of us?"

Perry pauses his speech and pats my hand. "Thank you for keeping me on track, Juliet." He gives me a patronizing smile before looking back at the waiter. "We'll have two plates of the Wagyu and the mixed vegetables."

"Right, that's what I had written down." The waiter almost manages to hide the snark from his words. "Can I get you ladies anything else to drink?"

Rosie and I shake our heads so the poor man can escape. With an internal sigh, I turn back to my "date" and ask a question I

pray will get us through another thirty minutes of this torture. "Have you ever been to Japan?"

First rule of making small talk with a pompous butthead—ask them questions that keep them talking about themselves.

"Ah…no, not yet. But I have studied the culture extensively, in fact I've even learned some of the language." Perry keeps talking about Japan, adding in some smug commentary about visiting Thailand next summer after graduation.

"They can keep him," Conner mutters, surprising a snort out of Rosie.

"Didn't you know, *shabu shabu* means 'I am an arrogant American' in every language except English?" Rosie whispers back. Conner chokes on his water, interrupting Perry mid-sentence.

"You should hit him on the back. Or if that doesn't work, you could give him the Heimlich." Perry points to Rosie, as if it's obvious that it's her job to take care of the coughing Conner. "As I was saying…"

Dinner drags on for an eternity. Even the fun of cooking paper-thin slices of beef in delicious miso broth is ruined by Perry's endless name dropping and explaining things as if we're toddlers. Perry touches my arm or my shoulder every time he feels a need to tell me something. Which is constantly. I can't help it that every time his fingers graze my skin my stomach turns over, but I manage to suppress my instinct to flinch away most of the time.

"Perry?" Rosie's sickly sweet tone stops him mid-sentence, saving me from the finer points of how Kobe beef is raised. "Whose idea was this…date?" She curls her lip in disgust at the word, but what else can this set-up be called but a blind double-date?

"After how successful our date was last week, I was happy to take you girls out again. Conner too." Perry pointed across the table with his chopsticks. Conner rolls his eyes, but doesn't contradict Perry.

"How do you consider that a success? The boys nearly pummeled you both," Rosie asks.

"No matter. I believe our fathers were all playing golf yesterday morning when the subject of your futures came up..." Perry's nose wrinkles in disgust. He accompanies this with a finger dragging across the back of my neck and this time I can't help pulling away, my own nose wrinkling as I shiver.

I shift in my seat, turning to face him but also pulling my body out of his reach. "What do you mean? Like college?"

Conner sighs, resting his chopsticks on his plate. "Mr. Caplan suggested you both needed to think about *who* you would be spending your futures with." Conner glances at Perry who's busy maneuvering a mushroom between his chopsticks to drop in the pot.

Rosie's face goes pale and she drops her chopsticks on the table. "What is this, *Bridgerton*? Are they seriously trying to sell us off to the highest bidder?"

The food I've eaten turns sour in my stomach.

Conner leans close and drops his voice. "I don't care what they want, I came to keep Perry from inviting one of his other country club friends. Trust me, you do not want to meet them." He shudders, fiddling with the tablecloth. "I'm sorry that you both got tricked into this, I had no idea until we got to your house and I saw your faces. I'm just here as your friend. If that's okay?"

Maybe this all would have been easier if I'd met Conner first. He seems nice enough, if a little bland. It would have been much safer to pick him to have a crush on instead of Romeo.

Just thinking about Romeo sends a wave of butterflies rioting through me. I never understood what he meant by having no control over who your heart falls for until I met him. I'd always been firmly in control of who I'd had crushes on, mainly fictional characters in my books. The way my heart was completely out of my control this summer, the way it just attached itself, willy-nilly, to the one boy it shouldn't have, was a revelation. I never knew I could feel anything as deeply as I know Romeo and I belong together.

Perry, oblivious to our conversation, keeps talking, as a white hot fire burns low in my belly. "I was thinking, tomorrow I'll come pick you up—"

"Shut the fuck up Perry." Rosie cuts him off, a fake smile plastered on her face.

"Excuse me?" The tips of Perry's ears turn red, his brow furrowed. "Did you just tell me to shut up?"

"Yes, I did." Rosie smirks. Conner and I glance at each other, eyes wide and fighting grins. "Jules and I had no idea what was happening tonight. If we'd known, I would have made sure to spoil our father's little plans in the most spectacular way possible."

Perry scoffs and opens his mouth to speak but Rosie glares him into silence and continues. "First of all, you keep talking as if the four of us are somehow a package deal, yet you're the only person who's making decisions. Did it ever occur to you that Conner might have his own thoughts on the matter? And most importantly, did you ever stop and ask yourself if Jules and I even wanted to be here? Or did you just assume that we would do whatever we were told?"

Across the table from me, Conner is grinning at Rosie's words. In fact, he seems to be eyeing her with a new respect. It's too bad he has no idea that he doesn't stand a chance with her.

"This isn't some kind of group deal, who exactly do you think you're dating? Me or Jules? Don't make me remind you of what happened last time you came near me with your lips."

Perry pales, leaning back in his seat, finally giving me some space. I don't know what that story is but I make a mental note to ask Rosie about it later—it sounds like I would enjoy it. "And if you think you're getting anywhere near Jules while Romeo or I have any life left in us, you're delusional."

Conner leans closer to interject. "I believe the plan, according to our parents, was that you and I would be together and Perry and Juliet would be a pair. Something about Principal St. Clair wanting Perry to get into the Foreign Service one day."

His confession startles a laugh out of me. "You think for one second I would want to be with someone who does exactly what my father does? I *hate* being dragged all over the world on someone else's whim. It sucks. As if I would ever volunteer for more of that life."

Perry's lip curls up. "Even if that's the case, you need to pick your friends more carefully. Who knows what could happen to you, associating with the likes of them."

"Hey, let's all just take a breath. Obviously our fathers are out of line trying to manipulate everyone here." Conner's attempt to make peace at the table would have worked if Perry didn't choose that exact moment to summon our server with the worst attempt at Japanese I've ever heard.

Our waiter doesn't notice, busy taking the order of a group across the room from us. Perry makes a whiney little moan, before muttering about the terrible service. "Perry, he obviously didn't hear you. Also, he probably doesn't speak Japanese." I point out the obvious.

"He works in a Japanese-style restaurant, why wouldn't he know the language?" Perry scoffs at me. My blood boils at his dismissive words.

"Um, probably because he's whiter than white, dude." Conner chimes in before I say something ugly. "Did you not notice the red hair and freckles?"

"You know what?" Perry starts, reaching into his pocket and pulling out his wallet. "This was supposed to be a nice evening. Conner and I could show you girls what it's like to be taken out to dinner by a gentleman instead of a hooligan." Perry drops some bills on the table and stands. "You should be grateful."

The three of us sit, dumbfounded, while he turns and walks out the door. "Shit, we gotta go, he drove." Conner hops up, glances at the cash on the table, and adds a couple of bills while Rosie and I gather our purses to follow him out the door.

"Perry!" Conner calls as we hurry through the door after him. "Wait up man." He jogs ahead. I follow a few steps, but jerk back as heated words float back to me. Rosie crashes into my back.

"Dude, let it go." Conner sounds like he's out of breath.

I pull Rosie between a couple of SUV's a few cars down from Perry's and crouch.

"They're a couple of fucking bitches, Conner. Can you believe them?" Perry's nasal tone is laced with contempt.

"Um what?"

I peek between the cars hiding us to see the look of disbelief on Conner's face.

Perry growls and throws a punch at a nearby tree, knocking leaves to the ground. "You're really going to put up with being treated like that? They're just girls who haven't been with a real man yet. They need someone to teach them a lesson."

Beside me, Rosie is vibrating with rage. "That son of a—"

I put a hand on her arm to stop her. Something about the way Perry said those words has me ready to run. "Shhh." I squeeze her arm to stop her from storming out there and throwing a punch. I don't *think* Perry would really hurt us, but I don't know for sure. He and Conner are still talking, but I can't make out their words over Rosie's hissing and spitting in my ear. All I know is, they sound angry.

I slip my phone out of my pocket and start typing.

ME: I need a knight in shining armor to come rescue me.

I attach our location and slip my phone back in my pocket without waiting for a reply. He'll come.

"...can't mess with me. I know people, I'm untouchable in this town." Perry's threats carry back to us and I freeze, the tinge of fear I'd felt before blossoming into full-blown panic.

"Let's just pick up the girls and take them home, Perry. They're probably waiting for us at the entrance." Conner's placating tone grates on me.

I nearly scream when Rosie whispers in my ear. "Please tell me you already texted Romeo?" I nod, afraid to make noise. Frozen, Rosie and I listen to the sound of two car doors opening and closing, then the engine roaring to life, my heart pounding.

Instead of slowing down and heading to the restaurant entrance, the engine picks up speed, before fading away. Rosie peeks over my head and swears. "He left! That asshole just took off and left us here!"

I pop up in time to see the taillights of Perry's car disappear around the corner, leaving Rosie and I stranded in the parking lot. I stare, shocked that he would actually just leave us here, when my phone buzzes.

> **TROUBLE:** On my way. Are you safe?
> **ME:** We're safe, just need a ride. Perry ditched us.

Romeo doesn't respond, but I assume he's driving. Rosie's phone, however, buzzes. She types a response, then laughs at something on the screen.

"What?"

Instead of telling me she hands over the phone so I can read it.

> **CONNER:** I am so sorry. Please tell Juliet I'm sorry. I swear I thought he was coming to get you guys.
> **ROSIE:** That was a pretty new low, even for him.
> **CONNER:** Judging by the throbbing vein about to explode on his forehead, maybe it's better that you girls aren't in the car with us right now. Shit, he's asking who I'm texting. Gotta go. Did you get a ride home? I can get my car and come back to get you if you need.
> **ROSIE:** I'm pretty sure our thugs are already on their way. Keep Perry far away or he might not survive his encounter with Juliet's savior. And no hard feelings, I know you're not the asshole. Feel free to kick Perry in the nuts for me though. And then once more for Jules.

"I want to do more than just kick him in the…" I mutter, half to myself, half to Rosie. Thirty seconds later, Rosie is getting into a particularly gruesome recipe for boiled *sausage* when Romeo's red Jeep comes flying into the parking lot. Dark hair messy and eyes wild, he's out of the car and wrapping his arms around me before I can speak. "Are you okay? Tell me you're okay. What did that asshole do?"

I let myself relax against his chest for a second, eyes closed, the tension in my body seeping out of me with each beat of his heart in my ear. "I'm fine. We're fine. Dinner was awful and he ditched us, that's all."

"Perry was being Perry. When we objected to the five-year-plan he and our parents concocted about our futures, he threw a tantrum. I'm pretty sure Conner is going to be the one who ends up the most traumatized from all of this," Rosie adds, shaking her head at Romeo while he checks over every inch of me. I don't know what he's looking for, but I let him turn me in a circle.

"Wait," I freeze, my back to him. I whirl to face him, face scrunched as my brain starts putting things together. "How did you get here so fast? It took us at least fifteen minutes to get here. I texted you…" I unlock my phone to check the time. "Two minutes ago."

A sheepish look replaces the fear on Romeo's face. His eyes dart from me to Rosie a few times while he rubs a hand on the back of his neck. "Ummm…I may have followed you when I saw you leaving with Perry and Conner."

Rosie smacks his arm. "You were spying on us?"

"Only a little bit. You know I can see your driveway from the den upstairs. I was watching a movie with the boys when I saw Perry and Conner pull up. Obviously, I wanted to know what Perry was doing at your house, *again*, so I watched. When I saw the look on your face." He reaches out to stroke my cheek, eyes worried. "I had to make sure you were okay."

In the back of my mind, Romeo following me while I went out with Rosie registers as something I should be wary of, but right now, I'm so relieved that he was close when I needed him that I push the thought away. Instead, I lean into his hand on my face. "Thank you for coming."

"I'll always come for you, Angel. Nothing could keep me away if you need me."

Maybe I should worry about the desperation I hear underneath those words, but tonight...tonight I don't care.

CHAPTER EIGHTEEN

Romeo

I HEAR HIM before I see him. Marcus emerges from the house singing at the top of his lungs, mashing up Nicki Minaj's *Anaconda* and Sir Mix-a-Lot's *Baby Got Back* for the benefit of the entire street. His sister Melody trails behind, cringing before she dashes to my car.

"Shut up, Marcus!" Melody smacks his arm as he swings into the front seat. "You were the one who said we had to be quiet." Crossing her arms, she scowls and settles into the back seat. I glance at her in the rear-view mirror. Her sharp cheekbones and aristocratic nose give her away as Marcus' sister, even before their matching golden blonde hair and blue eyes. She's only fifteen months younger than us, but a trick of birthday timing means that she's going into her sophomore year while we're headed into our senior year.

Of course, with an older brother like Marcus, having an extra year of cushion between them is for the best. Our teachers need the year to recover from Marcus before they take on Melody.

She's not as loud as him, but she gets shit done without anyone ever realizing it was her.

She scares me, to be honest.

"Did I say that, sister dearest?" He bats his eyelashes at her in the rear-view mirror. I catch a glimpse of her sticking her tongue out in response. "I merely meant that you shouldn't stomp down the stairs in those god awful shoes. You were giving me a headache."

"Ass."

Marcus twists in his seat to admire his own backside. "It's not quite America's, but it's making a good run at being classified as Oak Hills finest."

They bicker the whole drive, as usual, only stopping when I pull over onto the side of the gravel road we've been driving on for the last few miles. "Enough already, let's go." The air is cooler down here by the river, but that's not what has me impatient to get out of the car.

Juliet is waving at me from the edge of the water, the sun shining on her porcelain skin. Rosie, Benny, and Nikki are standing on the rocks near her—Benny and Nikki sneaking glances at each other behind Juliet's back. Steph and Fritz are on the other side of the creek, gathering firewood.

I don't hear Tia anywhere, interesting.

Grabbing the bag of snacks I stowed in my Jeep, I pick my way down the rocky bank to join them. Showing Jules all the best out of the way places in Oak Hills this summer has been magical. Making sure no one finds out that we're dating is harder than I expected. Juliet is terrified if we get caught she'll be sent back to her parents and I don't want to think what my dad would do to me if he found out.

But she's worth anything he could dish out.

The smile that lights up Juliet's face when I get close reminds me why I'm willing to risk everything for her. And the way she still makes my heart stop every time I kiss her? I'd jump through a thousand more hoops if that was my reward.

The moment I set my bag of snacks down, she's in my arms, hers wrapped around my neck and shoulders, her tiny body pressed against my chest. Bending down, I lose myself in the taste of her lips until the groans and whistles of our friends become too loud to ignore.

"Watching you play tonsil hockey was not part of the supportive friend agreement I signed," Benny teases. "Some of us just ate."

Juliet buries her face in my chest and more laughter rings out from the group.

"Ignore them Jules." Steph calls from across the creek. "They're just jealous. Right, babe?" Fritz calls out an agreement, his arms overflowing with the sticks Steph is piling on him. We did tease them for their PDA pretty mercilessly when they started dating.

Marcus and Melody sweep us up in their wake as we join our friends at the edge of the water. Melody makes a beeline for Rosie, whispering something in her ear that sets them both off in giggles. "Where's Tia?" Marcus asks Nikki as he approaches.

Nikki shrugs, sending a soft smile in Benny's direction. "Not here." When Benny smiles back, she ducks her head, fiddling with the hem of her shirt.

Marcus takes off to the clearing on the opposite bank, muttering about being a third wheel, while I enjoy being able to hold Juliet. We have the whole day to hang out here, no prying eyes to get us in trouble. It's been almost a month now, I think my friends are finally convinced that I'm serious about Juliet. They must be, since they keep covering for us.

I tip Juliet's chin towards me again, kissing the smile on her lips. "Hi, Beautiful." I pick her up and spin her in a circle, preserving this picture perfect moment in my mind for the future.

"Get a room!" Rosie's voice carries over the noise of the creek, accompanied by the sound of someone retching and giggling. Dragging myself away from Jules, a peek over her shoulder reveals Melody and Rosie standing on a pair of rocks, performing their disgust for everyone else.

"You are all more than welcome to go enjoy your afternoon elsewhere." I throw my arm over Jules shoulder, tucking her into my side and leading her away, a chorus of teasing following us.

They can tease as much as they want. I already knew that she had irrevocably become the center of my universe the night we met, in person, but every time I see her the feeling grows stronger. Like an invisible thread stitches us together a little bit tighter every time I look at her gorgeous face.

Threading her fingers through mine, Juliet leads me past some bushes and a curve of the creek. A few steps is all it takes for the trees and sound of the rippling water to muffle the noise of our friends. I find a flat rock and step out of my flip flops, the cool water calling to me. Sitting down on the rock, I stretch my legs out to let it run over my feet and calves, the relief from the heat instant. "Come here." Tugging gently, I pull Juliet between my knees, settling her against my chest, her delicate feet resting between mine as I take a second to breathe her in.

We sit in silence for a few moments, letting the water run past our toes. Her weight against my chest, my arms wrapped around her middle comfort me, taking the sting out of my mother's words as I left the house to pick up Marcus and Melody.

"I missed you." My words are buried in her neck as my lips trace a path along the smooth skin revealed by her high ponytail. "Everything is better when I'm with you." Juliet's laugh turns into a gasp as I run my tongue along the back of her ear.

"Romeo..." I can't tell if her sigh is encouragement or admonition, so I don't let up kissing my way from the back of her ear to the knobby ridge of her spine.

"Romeo." I ignore the warning in her tone and kiss my way across her back to her shoulder, my arms tightening around her waist. "What are we going to do?" Her question is a sigh as she melts against me, turning her face so I can capture her lips with mine.

I don't answer because I'm already lost in her. Nothing in the world is as important as this right here—this connection between two souls, two hearts, two star-crossed lovers sipping at each other's lips.

"I don't want to think about it, Jules. I just want to be here, in the moment." A tendril of worry snakes through my chest but I push it down, cut it off.

"But—" I don't let her finish the thought. I can't.

Minutes, or hours, pass by as we reacquaint ourselves with the taste and feel of each other. I push away the tug of worry that tries to distract me and focus on the beautiful girl in my arms. Her silky hair slips beneath my fingers as my hand grasps the back of her neck, the citrus scent of her lotion mixed with the coconut sunscreen she's slathered on. The warmth of her, the press of her ribs against my thigh with each gasp, the tangle of our feet in the water, little drops splashing up against our legs.

A hundred tiny sensations that are all wrapped up in the bliss of being here with her. The fear of what happens when our families find out only adds fuel to the fire burning in me when I think of her.

How can I do anything except spend every moment possible with Juliet? There's a very real clock ticking down our time together—every time my dad or her uncle comes home early we risk being caught. Every time she gets an email from her parents, I'm convinced they're going to tell her it's time to go back to Europe. Perry is a threat that hangs over my head and haunts my dreams. When I'm feeling particularly rational, I try to convince myself that she'd be better off with someone like Conner. Someone innocuous, someone safe, someone her parents would approve of.

But the thought of her with someone else rips me up inside. So I resign myself to living in the moment, to not think about the future, because the future is what terrifies me. The fear sits in my belly, waiting to pounce when I least expect it. One of these days it's going to catch me and I don't know what I'll do when it finally does.

CHAPTER NINETEEN

TROUBLE: Tree. Midnight.

ANGEL: Ummmmm…what?

TROUBLE: Meet me at the tree in your front yard
at midnight.

ANGEL: Why didn't you just say that?

TROUBLE: The walls have ears...

ANGEL: You're an idiot, you know that right?

TROUBLE: What fool this mortal be's!

ANGEL: That makes no sense but you're adorable so I
forgive you.

TROUBLE: You called me adorable! My life is
now complete.

DEAR JULIET,

Don't laugh, but I miss our letters. I miss the happiness I felt
when I saw your handwriting on a plain white envelope. I miss

looking to see what kind of stamp you used, where you'd sent it from. Even though I've seen you almost every day since you got here and we literally just got off the phone, it feels like I'll never run out of things to tell you.

Did you know the scar on my thumb is from the day Benny dared me to jump over the trash can at lunch freshman year? I would have made it, but there was a bit of broken plastic caught on the side and when I put my hand down to vault over the top, it caught the side of my thumb and sliced it open. The way you were rubbing your thumb over the scar during the movie made me remember how it happened. I have a lot of scars—most of them are from dumb shit I've done with Marcus and Benny. That scar on your knee...what's it from?

I'm really sorry for cancelling our plans last night. I fell asleep after we got home and I just couldn't get myself out of bed again. Do you forgive me?

—YOUR TROUBLE

> **ANGEL:** Did you seriously waste a stamp sending me a letter? Why didn't you just put it in the mailbox?
>
> **TROUBLE:** Good morning to you too, beautiful. Because it had to look like real mail not like it was coming from next door, just in case someone intercepted it.
>
> **ANGEL:** Intercepted? I feel like you're having too much fun with this spy business. But the letter was very sweet, I almost forgot what a thrill I used to get whenever I would get your letters.
>
> **TROUBLE:** You better write me back. I need a hit of that adrenaline.

ANGEL: I'll write back.

TROUBLE: Promise?

ANGEL: Cross my heart.

ANGEL: But I'm not wasting a stamp.

DEAR ROMEO,

I feel a little silly writing a letter when I can look out my window and see you sitting on your bed, on your phone. Hi. *waves lamely*

It is pretty romantic though. Writing letters, I mean. The idea of finding an old stack of them thrills me, but no one will ever find ours because truthfully I haven't kept all of them. Some of them I have, but not a lot of them. It's hard to justify keeping something like that when you're constantly moving.

But they weren't romantic anyway so I guess it's ok. I don't even know if these count since you didn't exactly write any sweet endearments in your last letter. You told me about your scar and stupid things you've done with the boys. But that's okay, we became friends through our mundane, trivial letters. Maybe that's what a good relationship is anyways, right? Just living through the mundane things together, punctuated by the odd moment of romance. I don't know—I've never done this before.

I haven't heard anything from my parents about going back at the end of summer, but my mom said they were hoping to be able to come out and visit in August. She didn't say when, and she didn't say if they were expecting me to go back with them.

Is it wrong of me to hope they let me stay?

That I hope I don't have to say goodbye to you and Rosie and everyone else? I've never had friends like this before. Friends I made myself, not people who happened to live in the area, or on the base, or the embassy compound. Kids my parents picked out for me to be friends with.

And of course there's you.

Stop pouting.

I know you're pouting right now. I can practically see your cute face. Your bottom lip would be stuck out, your eyebrows furrowed and those puppy dog eyes I can't resist would be looking up at me. You'd probably make that bottom lip quiver just so I'd feel guilty. It goes without saying that I want to stay because of you.

It's so obvious I don't have to say it. It's not a thought, it just *is*. You're the air I breathe, the sun on my skin, the breeze cooling the evening air. You can't see it, you don't know where it starts and where it ends. All you know is you'd die without it.

Juliet

ROSIE PULLS a different dress out of her closet, holding the hot pink fabric up and eyeing me. "Jules…Be careful, okay?" Shaking her head, she put it back without letting me touch it, trading it for a dark blue dress a few inches longer.

I force myself not to roll my eyes and groan. She's just being protective, but I'm so sick of everyone treating me like an idiot, like I don't know how to be a teenager. "We know what we're doing, Rosie. We're going all the way to Lakewood. It's twenty miles away—who could possibly know us there?" I reach out for the blue dress in her hands. "Besides, it's just dinner, what can possibly go wrong?"

"Don't say that out loud, girl. You know that's exactly when something terrible is going to happen." Rosie raps her knuckles against the wooden closet door, shaking her head as I hold the dress up against my body. It's a cute dress, but cute isn't what I was going for tonight. If I'd just wanted cute I would have worn something of my own.

"Not that one, it's too sweet." Shaking my head, I hand the dress back. "You're as bad as my mom, quit babying me."

"You take that back right now you little shit." Laughing, she hangs the dress back up and pulls out a pink dress from the back of her closet. "Don't come crying to me when this all goes bad. I tried to warn you."

"Rosie, I know you're just trying to watch out for me, but would it kill you to be happy for us? It's been almost two months and nothing has happened." I slip the dress over my head and down my hips. "Eventually, when my parents and yours see that us being together has been nothing but good, they'll have to be okay with it. Right?"

Rosie bites her bottom lip, looking me up and down. I swing from side to side, the loose dress flaring out from my shoulders. "You say that like our parents are reasonable. You and I both know they'll never be rational when it comes to the Montgomerys." She shakes her head and indicates I should give the dress back. "They'll never see them as anything but money-grabbing leeches, and they'll never see Romeo as anything but the kid who used to steal their newspapers and ride his bike up and down the street with his gang of friends, yelling at the top of his lungs."

I pull the dress over my head, grinning at my cousin as I hand it back. "He still does, just with his Jeep instead of a bike." I step around her to flick through the hangers in her closet, stopping when I get to a red dress I've never seen.

"What about this one?"

"Juliet Caplan, did you just voluntarily pick out the shortest dress in my closet? I'm so proud." Rosie claps her hands, bouncing on her toes as I hold the dress up against my body. "Look at you, showing off those legs. And don't even get me started on that low back."

I pull the dress over my head, the tight fit unfamiliar, but not uncomfortable. I turn to look in her full-length mirror. The neckline is pinched into a sweetheart, the ripples of fabric making my boobs look fuller than usual, the spaghetti straps of the dress doing nothing to dispel the illusion. Soft, jersey fabric hugs my torso, leaving nothing to the imagination, stopping just above the middle of my thighs, a frilly ruffle at the bottom keeping it from being indecently short. "How do I look?"

Rosie gapes at my reflection. "Like Romeo is going to pass out when he sees you from the sudden lack of blood flowing to his brain. I almost don't know if I can let you go out in that, my parents might finally realize I've fully corrupted you." But instead of taking back the dress, Rosie rummages around in her closet, emerging with a pair of heels so high just looking at them makes my ankles ache.

The camel-colored leather straps wrap around my ankles, holding the heels on securely. I have no idea if I'll be able to walk in them, but they make my legs look amazing.

"We're only young once, right?" I twist from side to side, admiring the outfit in the mirror. My heart picks up speed at the thought of what my trouble-maker of a boyfriend is going to do when he sees me. "Something about being with Romeo makes me feel a little wild, a little out of control." I grin at her reflection. "I like it."

Rosie's eyes go wide at my words. "Who are you and where is the perfectly behaved Juliet who got off the plane two months ago? I gotta say, I like this version. Although, you still freak out when I drive five miles over the speed limit."

I would protest but she's not wrong.

"But I like that you are doing things that *you* want to do, even if it's not what our parents think you should do. Although I *still* don't trust Romeo..."

"*I* trust him."

"That's what scares me."

CHAPTER TWENTY-ONE

Romeo

THE FOG of apathy I've been fighting all day finally clears as I step up to the Caplan's front door. I'm annoyed at myself for not being more excited about tonight, but the darkness is tugging at me today, tempting me to crawl back into my bed and sleep until next week.

I should be eager to take Jules out, not forcing myself to take the last three steps to her house. Not when I've finally convinced her to let me take her out to a fancy dinner. Granted, I had to promise that we would drive all the way to Lakewood, but I'd do anything to make her feel more comfortable. We're going to go get lost in the crowd of the bigger city and enjoy not having to sneak around and watch our backs for once.

I opt to send Jules a text to let her know I'm at the front door, rather than knock. I don't see Chuck or Cathy's cars, but I'm not taking any risks tonight.

BENNY: Just be careful. I don't have bail money.

MARCUS: I can't believe I'm about to say this, but I agree. Be careful.

ROMEO: Awww, I didn't know you both cared so much! Orange is not my color though, I promise to be somewhat well-behaved.

Pocketing my phone as the lock clicks, I choke at the vision that swings it open. The red dress that hugs Juliet's body dips and curves over her. My palms itch to touch her. "Uh....wow. Jules..."

Rosie smirks. "Told you. Try not to swallow your tongue, Romeo."

"Be nice Rosie." Jules throws a grin over her shoulder at her cousin, giving me a chance to admire the way the back of the dress hugs her hips and ass, the ruffly bit at the bottom teasing the skin of her thigh. I'm trying to be a gentleman, but that dress is lighting up every single cell of my lizard brain.

Instead of the animal sounds that want to come out, I swallow them down and force real English to leave my lips. "Hey. You look nice." They were lame words, but better than the gorilla grunts that are making up my internal dialogue at the moment. This was definitely worth getting out of bed.

I will never admit this to Marcus, but Melody helped me pick out my outfit tonight. The dark jeans and solid maroon button down were my choice, but she insisted I roll up the sleeves and add a vest. I wasn't going to argue with her, but by the appreciative look on Juliet's face I should send her flowers as a thank you or something.

Another beat passes, Jules and I drinking each other in while Rosie stands back, trying to glare at me but with a grin threatening to take over her face. I swallow hard and try to speak again, this time the right words fighting their way through the fog of wanting to wrap Jules up in my arms. "I think my heart just stopped. Before tonight, I never knew what true beauty was, never felt my heart ache from it before now. You've never looked more like your name, Angel."

I can't help the tears that prick at my eyes, or the way my throat tightens at the sight of her. My Angel is so breathtaking, she'd make the devil weep. "God, you're so beautiful, what did I do to deserve someone like you?" Of it's own free will, my hand reaches up to stroke her cheek, her skin so soft I don't want to stop, especially when a pink blush creeps under my fingers. "I must have been a monk in another life."

Rosie laughs at me, pulling us both out of the trance we're in. "If I didn't know better, I'd say you actually meant that."

I make a face at her, sticking out my tongue, an action that would have gotten me a smack upside the head from my dad, or hers, in our youth. These days it would get me a lot worse but I don't care. Juliet standing in front of me shines a light into my soul that makes everything feel easier, brighter, like the world is worth living in. Arguing with Rosie is just how we are, we always have been, it's how we show each other we care. Tyson gave up on being the referee between us years ago.

"Don't be jealous, Rose."

Smirking, Jules smacks me on the shoulder and I grin down at her beautiful face. "I'm kidding, I'm kidding. You'll cover for us, right?"

"Yeah, yeah. But I swear on everything holy, if you hurt her I will castrate you, fry your balls in butter, and feed them to you, Marcus and Benny." The glee with which she threatens me should worry me. It doesn't, because I would never hurt my Angel. But it should.

"What did Marcus and Benny do to you?"

"They encourage your nonsense."

I grin. "Pretty sure half the nonsense we got up to as kids was your idea."

Arguing with Rosie is like putting on my favorite, oldest, t-shirt. It's comfortable, puts me at ease, and even though I know I shouldn't default to it all the time, I can't help myself. The things Juliet does to my heart has me reaching for the comfort of bantering with Rosie, even just for a minute, to ground myself. I need that familiarity, to remind myself of who I am.

Before Rosie and I can really get going, Jules tugs on my arm, stomping one foot like an adorable cartoon fairy. "Dammit, I was promised a real date. You two can argue later." Her cheeks turn pink at the swear, Rosie's mouth, hanging open at the unexpected word coming from her lips, matching mine. "Every time I've seen you in the last few weeks we've been in a group. If I'm going to break the rules, I'm going to really break them." She grabs my hand, pulling me away from Rosie. "You can threaten him later. We need to go before someone sees us."

The reminder that all of this could be taken away if the wrong person sees us snaps something in my brain. No matter how warm and bright Jules is, it's not enough to defeat the cold, dark cloud that hovers on the edge of my thoughts. One reminder is all it takes for the sun to disappear.

We've gone a handful of wobbly steps before I scoop her up in my arms and run to my car. Maybe if I hold tight enough, her light will push away the cold that snuck up on me. I only put her down briefly to open the door. I put the door panels back in this afternoon, figuring my Angel wouldn't want to mess up her hair on the long drive to Lakewood.

Laughing, she clings to my shoulders and I sink into the rightness of how she feels there. Her soft giggles in my ear send my heart into overdrive and lights my skin on fire, burning away the dark. When she presses a soft kiss below my ear, the blood leaves my head so fast I stumble.

"Don't do that if you want to make it there in one piece. I can't think straight when you kiss me." I growl my words out, even as I'm grinning down at her.

My angel just smiles at me. "I'm not sorry. I kinda like this feeling, like I could bring you to your knees if I wanted." I help her climb on the front seat of my Jeep. She grabs my cheeks and pulls me in for a kiss before I can walk around to my side. Her kiss is hungry, tugging and pulling at me, pouring herself into the meeting of our lips, just like I'm pouring myself right back.

Pulling back while I still can, I rest my forehead against hers. "We should go. You ready for this?"

Touching her lips to mine in the lightest of kisses, Juliet smiles. "With you? I'm ready for anything."

CHAPTER TWENTY-TWO

Juliet

MY STOMACH gurgles around the delicious food stuffed inside it. Or maybe it's nerves from the question that has been on the tip of my tongue all night. I don't know why I'm so nervous to ask him. But my stomach is twisting in knots and my fingers restlessly scrunch the thick cloth napkin in my lap. He was so quiet on the drive here, his silence makes me nervous.

"Is everything okay?" The question leaks out of me as the waiter walks away with our empty plates. He's lost to sight in the dim lighting moments later. When we got here, I suspected Romeo picked this place especially because it seems designed for privacy in the way that only really expensive restaurants are. The back of the booth we're in is high, hiding us from sight, and the lights are low. Apart from an initial bit of doubt that a couple of teenagers had reservations here and not down the street at the Olive Garden, no one has paid any attention to us apart from our waiter. It's perfect.

Romeo puts his water glass down on the table, eyeing me. "What do you mean?"

"I mean...When you picked me up everything was fine. We were joking with Rosie. And then...it's like you turned off. You've barely said a word to me all night. Did I say something wrong?"

"Because I'm not being my usual loud and obnoxious self?" Romeo's question is quiet, but I don't trust he's not going to explode at me for questioning him. Is he angry? I shouldn't have asked. Was it selfish of me to think tonight was special? The twisted napkin unravels in my lap.

"No, that's not what I want, not what I mean. You're not obnoxious. I just..."

He exhales, his shoulders drooping. "Sorry. My dad laid into me last night. I forgot to unload the dishwasher, again. Which turned into him listing all my faults." The dishwasher, all this is about the dishes?

"Sometimes I can't help thinking he's right, Jules. That I'm just like my mom, a waste of space." His dark eyes are pained, looking past me at nothing and everything. "I don't want to believe your family is right about mine...but what if they are?"

I suck in a steadying breath, hating how my voice is getting squeaky. "They're wrong. I don't know what happened and I really wish someone would just tell me why our families hate each other so much, but they have to be wrong about you."

Romeo doesn't answer me for a moment. Emotions pass in rapid succession over his expressive face—confusion, sadness, resignation. He scrubs both hands over his cheeks, like he's bracing himself to deliver bad news. What can possibly be so terrible that he's this anxious to tell me?

The long silence drags on, every second piling more guilt on my heart for asking the question. This is what I get for being so sheltered, so inexperienced—I can't even ask a simple question without getting it all wrong.

Romeo pushes his goblet of water to the side, reaching his hand across the table. Silent, he picks up my fingers, feeling and touching each one, eyes focused down, blinking rapidly.

"Romeo?" My instinct is to smooth it over, apologize, take it back, say whatever I need to say to spare his feelings. Just like my mom would, like *I* do when my dad is angered by something. Isn't that what you do for your person? You smooth things over for them, keep them happy at all costs. That's what love is, right? Loving your person more than you love yourself.

I'm about to open my mouth and tell him it doesn't matter, I don't need to know and I'm sorry for asking him something painful, when Romeo speaks.

"Angel, there's something I need to tell you. About why our parents hate each other so much. And about me." He stops, takes a deep breath and looks up. There's so much pain in the dark depths of his eyes. Pain so deep, so ingrained, it isn't about me. "About a month after we moved into your old house, my mom was going down into the basement to put some stuff away when one of the steps gave way and she fell."

"Was she seriously hurt?" I've seen his mom, she doesn't seem injured. A little distracted and out of touch, but physically fine.

"She broke her leg and was pretty sore for a couple of weeks."

That's it? This doesn't make sense. "But why does a broken leg ten years ago mean our parents hate each other so much? I kind of remember something about an issue with the house, but my parents would never talk to me about that kind of thing."

My parents never talk to me about anything. They just conduct regular inquisitions. The only thing they want to know is how I'm doing with my schoolwork. "If it doesn't concern school they don't care," I add when Romeo slouches back in his seat, pulling his hand free from mine.

"You know my dad's a lawyer, right? I know your uncle's probably called him an ambulance chaser or something like that, right?" He won't meet my eyes as he speaks, looking anywhere but at me.

I can't deny it, Uncle Chuck has called Romeo's dad a lot of names, ambulance chaser being one of the nicer ones.

There's another long pause before Romeo speaks. This time I don't try to fill the silence, I wait. He swallows hard, fiddles with his goblet, drums his fingers on the table. Willing myself to be patient, I take a careful sip from my own water goblet, the cold liquid taking some of the edge off the heat in my cheeks. "My mom was pretty banged up, so the doctors sent her home from the hospital with a lot of painkillers. But, well…She couldn't stop taking them, even after her leg was healed. She's functional, most of the time, but the problem's never really gone away."

As soon as the words settle in my brain, lightbulbs start clicking on one by one. The way he never invited us over. Why no one talks about his mom or asks about her. The stories they've told me about him sneaking over for dinner all the time. The times I've looked out the window late at night or early in the morning and seen someone pacing around the house, TV flickering, lights on at all hours.

I almost miss Romeo's confession, I'm so busy cataloguing the behaviors I'd seen but hadn't really noticed. "Anyway, my dad blames your parents and he took it out on them by suing for damages."

"Romeo…" Tears well up in my eyes as I reach across the table.

He squeezes my hand, but doesn't look at me. "Don't. Please don't look at me like that."

I squeeze back before pulling my hand free to twist the napkin in my lap again. "Why don't I remember any of this?"

"I don't know. I know they never actually went to court. That's not all."

I wait, lacing my fingers through his.

"My house—" He stops, swallows and starts over. "I know your aunt and uncle aren't exactly the greatest, but compared to mine…well, they might as well be perfect. The reason Rosie and I, and Tyson, became such good friends was because I hated to be at my own house. You remember my very first letter?"

"Of course." I smile. "I kept that one."

"I didn't actually lose a bet with Rosie. She made me write the letter as payback for not letting her be the first to sign my cast. I wasn't trying to climb the tree outside her window."

My eyebrows scrunch as confusion settles in. "What do you mean? What happened then?"

"She caught me trying to sleep in the tree in my backyard."

"What? Why on Earth were you trying to sleep in a tree? You wrote me that letter in October, wasn't it freezing?" I don't understand what all of this has to do with me or why Romeo is having such a hard time telling me this story.

"I was sleeping out there because my dad locked me out of the house."

"On accident?" I don't understand, why would his father do that?

"No. He came home from work late and I asked him what was for dinner. He told me to ask my mom, but she had been passed out in her bed all afternoon. He lost his temper, told me I was 'old enough to make a fucking pb&j', then locked me out of the house all night to teach me a lesson." He stops to take a shaky breath. "So, I tried to sleep in a tree, fell out and had to go to the emergency room. My mom perked up enough to come with me and make sure they prescribed me pain medication, which she kept."

"I bet your dad was really mad," I whisper. I've heard Mr. Montgomery yelling at someone once or twice, I can only imagine how scary it would be to have someone like that mad at me.

"He didn't speak to me for a week."

Romeo's tone is flat, cold. I want to slide into the booth next to him, wrap my arms around him and tell him that I would never do that. That I would never treat him like that.

"There's something else I need to tell you." Romeo doesn't make eye contact with me, drawing in the condensation on the side of his water glass instead. "When we were fourteen…" He swallows and looks up. I give him a watery smile, hoping he'll keep going.

"Those were some hard years for me. Perry and his buddies would constantly harass me about my mom and the crap their parents used to say about mine. I wasn't as close with Marcus and Benny as I am now, so I was pretty easy prey for them."

"But what about…?" I don't even know what I'm trying to say, just that my heart is breaking for the part of himself Romeo kept hidden all those years.

He shakes his head and attempts to smile. "There was one night…I just couldn't take it anymore Angel. I just wanted everything to be over, I was so tired of fighting my way through the day."

I gasp, an inkling of where this is going dawning on me.

"I found my mom's stash…"

"That was real?" That letter, the one that had scared me, the one where he talked about his mom's pills. I hadn't really believed he was serious, that someone our age would want to end their life, that they wouldn't want to know what came next. I always wanted to know what came next. "Did you…did you write that letter before or after?"

"About five minutes before." His confession weighs heavy in the air. I don't know what to say. We sit in silence while I digest that the strange letter he'd sent me all those years ago had almost been the last one. "And I didn't actually take them, Angel. I just…thought about it for a really long time. In the end I just took one to see what it was like. I wanted to know what was so great about them. Why my mom loved her pills more than me. No one would have known if I hadn't let it slip when I was having dinner at the Caplan's one night. That was the last night I was allowed over."

"But this was all years ago. And why didn't you tell me any of this sooner?" A touch of anger builds in my belly, right next to the overwhelming sadness I feel for Romeo and my confusion over being kept in the dark. Once again, naive Juliet is the last to know, the innocent baby who has to be spared from anything distasteful. Why? Because I'm too fragile to handle it? Why didn't he tell me? "I don't know what to say. I wish you'd trusted me enough to tell me sooner."

The hurt in my voice gets Romeo's attention. His eyes finally snap to meet mine, anguish written all over his face. "No, no, no, Angel. It wasn't like that. You have to believe me." He's begging, tugging on my hand but now it's my turn not to meet his eyes. I'm too hurt at being left in the dark. He moves, sliding into the booth next to me, grabbing both of my hands in his. "I didn't want to tell you because...well. I didn't want you to look at me differently."

"Are you, um, okay now?" My question is quiet, but in our little bubble, the words echo in my ears.

Romeo squeezes my hand again. "Yeah. I'm okay now. Well, mostly okay. I still have bad days, like I told you, but having you in my life has made everything better."

"You've heard how your aunt and uncle talk about my parents—the drug addict, the scumbag lawyer and their screw-up kid. That's how everyone in town sees us. White collar low-lifes. Too rich to shun, but too crass for polite society. You think I don't know exactly what they think of my family? I know what people like the St. Clairs say about us behind our backs. I bet they told you to stay away from me, right? That my family was a 'bad influence'?"

I can't deny it.

"I just can't bear the thought of you looking at me like every-one else does." It's the crack in his voice on the last word that breaks me, pulls me from my confusion long enough to see the distress he's in.

Another light bulb goes off in my head. "You don't want me to see you the same way as everyone else does. That's why you didn't tell me. Because you're afraid that I'll leave you if I know the real you?"

"Terrified." One word, that's all it takes for my anger to melt away. I melt into him, my head on his shoulder. Relief floods through me as his arms wrap around me, holding me close.

"I *do* know the real you and I'm not going anywhere."

A heavy hand on my shoulder and a familiar voice have me freezing like a deer caught in headlights. "That's exactly what I was afraid of."

I sit up and peer over the back of my seat, to find myself looking into the faces of the last two people I expected to see tonight. "Mom? Dad? What are you...?"

Romeo bolts up from his spot next to me, standing rigidly at the end of the table, the shock on his face matching my own. "Sir—"

But my father doesn't give him a chance to explain, cutting him off with a tug on my bicep. "Be quiet, boy. Juliet, we're leaving. Now."

I pull back, confusion ripping through me. "Dad, no."

He pulls on my arm again, hurting me. I wince and Romeo makes a choking noise. "I don't understand, when did you guys get here?"

My parents ignore my question, instead looking around the restaurant and lowering their voices. "The St. Clair kid was right, looks like we got here just in time."

My mom's words don't carry, but I can hear them just fine. Romeo can too, judging by the way his eyebrows furrow. "Juliet, stand up, we are leaving. Now."

"No." I'm not sure who's more shocked by my absolute refusal—me, my parents or Romeo. Or possibly Uncle Chuck and Aunt Cathy, who I now see hovering behind my mom, faces turning tomato red.

I tune out the shocked sputterings and words of my four supposed guardians, my eyes locked on Romeo's instead. He raises one eyebrow in acknowledgement of my words before glancing at the adults behind me. My dad's grip is painfully tight on my arm. I try to pull it free but he doesn't let go.

"Sir, I don't mean to be disrespectful, but—" Romeo's words cut through their angry buzz.

It's my Uncle Chuck who turns on him, loud enough to hush the conversations around us, a beefy arm pushing Romeo into the seat across from me. "No, you listen to me young man. You and your parents are just a bunch of trailer trash in designer clothes. I thought I made it clear years ago that my girl was off limits to scum like you. What would make you think my niece was any different? It was one thing to allow you in our house when your own mother couldn't be bothered to feed you—"

Now that I know the whole story, I can't stop the rage that fills me at Chuck's words. How dare he throw that in Romeo's face? "—but I thought you understood your place in this world. And now I catch you taking what doesn't belong to you? You'll never deserve her, never be good enough for anyone, let alone my family. I should have known you were as rotten as your parents."

Each word out of Uncle Chuck's mouth slams into Romeo with sniper-like accuracy. My heart breaks as Romeo crumbles at the attack. After his confession, I know that each word is burrowing deep into the soft core he hides from everyone except me.

I'm trying to reach out, to hold his hand, share some of my own strength against their words but Aunt Cathy and my mom are tugging at me, trying to pull me out of my seat. Romeo sits there, eyes down, taking the verbal blows being dealt him by my father and uncle without ever raising a voice to protest, to stand up for himself. Before my eyes, he turns meek and cowed. I hate it. I can't stand to see what they're doing to my bright, funny, over the top love.

Aunt Cathy and my mom are arguing over my head, attacking each other as much as they're admonishing me. Uncle Chuck and Dad are leaning down, whispering furiously to Romeo. His cheeks are pale, shaking his head from side to side, his mouth opening like he wants to speak but they don't give him a chance to get a word in.

"Come on Juliet, we're leaving." My mom's sharp tone would have had me scrambling to my feet a few weeks ago. Instead I stay put, digging down into the booth.

"Get up, right now young lady." Aunt Cathy is easier to ignore.

I pull my arms free of their grip and cross them over my chest. "I'm staying." I hate the waver in my voice, but I have no practice at this. For a first time, I think I'm doing pretty well at disobeying orders.

My mom isn't having any of it. She leans down to hiss in my ear. "You've had your little rebellion, but it's done now. Get. Up."

Aunt Cathy moves to speak to the men allowing my mom to get a good look at my dress. She whirls on Cathy, her wrath finding a new target. "You let her leave the house dressed like this?"

"What the hell are you wearing?" Cathy passes the attack back to me, eyeing my dress.

Feeling smug, I uncross my arms, draping one on the back of the booth. "I borrowed it from Rosie."

I turn to look at Romeo, but he's not grinning like I hoped. My momentary triumph disappears at the look on his face. He's pleading with his eyes for me to stop fighting them, to stop making it worse.

"Move. Now." My dad's words are punctuated by an implacable grip on my shoulders. I wriggle, trying to get loose but it's no use. I can't escape his hands, I can't escape his rules or the life he and my mom have mapped out for me. Just enough education to make the perfect wife one day. Just pretty enough to look good on someone's arm. Pliable. Subservient. No dreams of my own, just a footnote in someone else's life.

Something inside me snaps. If I don't break free now I never will, I'll never get to make my own choices, never get to live the life I choose. I fight against my father's hands, pulling away, pushing him off me. "No! No, stop! I'm not leaving. Romeo!"

Desperate, I reach across the table for the boy who lit the spark inside of me, but he doesn't reach back and my heart cracks in two. Whispers carry toward us, other diners are staring, their eyes hot and judging on my skin.

There's a threat in my uncle's tone as he leans down to whisper in my other ear. "Stop making a scene. What is wrong with you?"

Aunt Cathy wrings her hands uselessly, eyes darting around the restaurant. "See what a bad influence he's been on you? This is exactly what I knew would happen."

I ignore them, my eyes glued to the boy who holds my heart across the table from me. He won't meet my eyes. "Romeo, do something. Say something—anything. Help me!" My words echo in a sudden silence. No one speaks, waiting for Romeo to say something.

Finally, he looks up, those dark eyes meeting mine, glistening with tears. "Maybe they're right, you should go. You deserve better than someone like me."

He doesn't mean it, he can't.

"Romeo?" My chest tight, I can't get a full breath. My hand flies across the table, knocking over both of our water glasses but I don't care. I need to touch him, need him to reassure me that he doesn't mean it. "Please?" Tears drip down my cheeks, I didn't even know I'd started crying.

Mute, he glances up at Uncle Chuck, looks at me and shakes his head. "You should go.

Shocked, numb, no one moves. I'm stretched half across the table, reaching for him. Throats clear behind me but I ignore them. "Don't do this, don't let them win," I whisper, my words catching on a sob. Romeo stares at my hand, his own just inches away. For a moment, I think he's going to ignore me, but then he leans in close, taking my cheeks in both of his hands, pressing a desperate kiss to my own desperate lips. He's whispering against my lips but I can't make out the words through my own sobs. I just know I can't let them take him away from me.

Rough hands haul me away, inescapable. Someone drapes a sweater over my shoulders and an arm around my waist holds me hostage. A manager comes hurrying over. "Excuse me, I'm going to need you to take this discussion outside, you're disturbing the other guests."

Uncle Chuck and Dad are arguing with the manager, but my eyes are trained on Romeo. Silently, he pulls cash out of his wallet and lays it on the table. Look at me, just look at me, my heart begs. But he doesn't.

Shoulders slumped, he pushes back from the table and walks away. A new emotion I've never felt before creeps over me. They broke him. Heat of a new kind spreads across my skin and I see red. "Let go, stop it." I try to yell but it comes out a broken whisper. "Look at him, look at what you've done!" Someone is telling me to calm down, to be quiet, to settle down. I won't. I'll never calm down again if they don't let me go, let me fix what they broke. Fix my Romeo's heart, his soul, the light in him they just snuffed out with their cruel words.

My eyes are glued to his back. I will him to look back. Look back just once, see me fighting, see how I'm fighting for him, for us.

Romeo pauses at the door, and the sounds of arguing and telling off the manager with stupid phrases like "do you know who I am?" fade. We lock eyes across the room, and another sob escapes me as I renew my struggle against the hands holding me. He's giving up. He doesn't believe he's worth fighting for.

The door closes behind him and the rage and despair burning in my gut explode out of me. "What's wrong with you?" I'm shouting, the words ripped from the depths of my broken heart. "How could you say that to him? You don't know anything about him, you don't know him. He's not what you think!" My skull is pounding at the force of my cries. "I hate you! I hate you all!"

My dad scoffs, Aunt Cathy and Uncle Chuck sputter, and my mom gasps. The sound snaps whatever bit of rational thought I had left in me. They'll never understand—nothing I say will change their minds. "I love him and I don't care what you think." I wrench free of their grip and race across the restaurant, sobs wracking my body as I push past chairs and tables. I slam through the door, barreling straight into Romeo outside.

Romeo catches me before I fall, his arms wrapping around me, soothing the fear that he'd left me behind. "What are you doing?" The tremble in his voice adds another crack to my battered heart, but I push it away for now.

Glancing back at the adults pushing their way through the restaurant towards us, desperation pushes me to speak without caring about the consequences for the first time in my life. "I'm doing what *I* want for once. Now, are you going to drive or what?"

I grab Romeo's hand and we race towards his Jeep. We're almost there when I step on a large rock and stumble. I hit the asphalt, sharp pain stinging the skin of my palms and knees. Romeo helps me to my feet and we keep running. "I'm fine, I'm fine," I reassure him before he can ask. There's gravel stuck in my skin and I can feel something dripping down my right knee, but I don't stop. The crash of the restaurant door behind us and shouts from adults who would do anything to keep us apart, spur me on.

We get to his Jeep, but Romeo stops me before I can scramble onto the seat. "Are you sure? About me?" Tears fall from his eyes just like mine.

Eyes wide, Romeo stares at me. There's no going back now, and we both know it. We've jumped off a cliff together, no idea what's waiting for us at the bottom.

Romeo grabs my face and pours everything into a kiss, our tears mingling. "I love you more than life itself. Living without you isn't an option. If I can't have you in my life, I don't want it."

I grab his vest and slam my mouth to his in answer. Pulling back, I speak the words that burned through me as we ran, hot tears streaming down my face. "Romeo Montgomery, I love you. I don't care what anyone says, they don't know you like I know you."

CHAPTER TWENTY-THREE

ROSIE: Hey, are you guys ok? Mom, Dad and your parents just showed up at the house and they are PISSED. What happened? Also, when did your parents get here?

ROSIE: Spill! I want to know the drama. I know it's juicy.

ROSIE: Hello?

ROSIE: Jules? Romeo? Do you not have reception?

ROSIE: You both owe me big time, I just got grounded and basically locked in my room because they think I know where you are and I'm not spilling. What the fuck you guys? This isn't cool.

ROSIE: Ok, this isn't funny, where the hell are you guys? It's been hours and no one's heard from you. They're calling the police.

MARCUS: Have you heard anything?

BENNY: Heard what?

MARCUS: From lover boy. According to Rosie they got caught by her folks and split. Have you heard from them?

BENNY: No, I haven't. Has anyone tried locating their phones?

MARCUS: That's why you're the brains of this operation.

MARCUS: No dice. You?

BENNY: Nothing. Shit. This is bad. I'll keep looking.

ROSIE: Has anyone heard from Jules or Romeo? TL:DR they went out on a date and got caught by my folks, there was a lot of yelling and then they took off. No one's seen or heard from them in hours. If anyone hears anything please tell me!

NIKKI: I haven't heard anything, but I'll let you know if I do.

MELODY: OMG, that's so scary! I haven't heard anything. Are you ok?

ROSIE: I'm fine right now. Mostly pissed that I'm the one locked in my room until they find the lovers. But I'm a little worried, this is so unlike Jules.

MELODY: I would have thought that she would at least tell YOU something. If Marcus hears anything I'll let you know.

TIA: Haven't heard. I'm sure they'll show up in the morning or something. They probably just want to give everyone a good scare.

STEPH: Tia! What if something happened to them? What if they got in a car accident or something? Has anyone called the local hospitals?

ROSIE: I don't know, they won't tell me anything. Hang on, I can hear something downstairs…

BENNY: I think I found something.
MARCUS: Don't be a dick, tell me.
BENNY: I was listening to the police scanner radio and there's a report of an accident on the highway between here and Lakewood.
MARCUS: Fuck. Do you think it's them?
BENNY: It's a red Jeep. Two passengers, both being airlifted to Lakewood General.
BENNY: …
BENNY: …
MARCUS: What aren't you telling me, man?
BENNY: Being airlifted to the hospital is a really bad sign.

STEPH: Rosie! What's happening, you left us hanging twenty minutes ago.
NIKKI: Rosie? What's going on?
TIA: This is killing me, someone please tell me what's going on.
MELODY: Marcus thinks they found them.
NIKKI: They found them? That's good, right?
STEPH: That's a relief!
TIA: Drama's over? Can we all go to bed now?

STEPH: Tia, don't be a bitch, I can hear you making TikToks over there.

NIKKI: Tia, Steph, shut up. Melody? Where were they?

MELODY: Marcus says he and Benny think they got in a car accident and airlifted to a hospital in Lakewood, that's why no one knew it was them at first. Rosie just texted to tell me she was on her way there with her parents. Marcus is going to take me to go see them tomorrow, if they'll let us.

MELODY: Guys, if you pray, pray for them. It doesn't sound good.

CHAPTER TWENTY-FOUR

Romeo

"ANY WORD on our Romeo?"

Everything hurts.

Juliet's hand in mine, squeezing tight as she sobs and laughs at the same time.

Head pounding from the incessant beeping.

"Not that I've heard. How's the girl?"

Juliet's head on my shoulder, my arm wrapped around her as we drive.

Someone moves my arm, cold washes through me.

Bright lights, highlighting the tear-tracks on Juliet's cheeks.

"Hey Paula, the officer who found them needs to talk to you. Your patient in four fifteen needs more pain meds, too."

"I'll be right there. Okay honey, you gotta fight for me now, okay? Don't you give up on me."

Warm.

Quiet.

Peace.

The pain floats away from me as I sink into the dark depths of nothing.

CHAPTER TWENTY-FIVE

Juliet

I'M LAUGHING *and crying, tears splashing down my face even though I'm wiping them away with the back of my hand.*

Why am I laughing?

I should be terrified.

My cheeks sting from the rough wiping.

My whole body aches.

"There's napkins in the glove compartment, Angel."

Napkin in my hand, my head resting on Trouble's shoulder. I should be terrified, but all I feel is safe.

Trouble.

My Trouble.

I've gotten us both in trouble now.

I said the word I've never said to them in my life.

No.

I won't.

You can't make me.

Can they?

Of course they can.
I'm so tired.
Bright lights, highlighting the worry in Romeo's eyes.
What are we going to do?
What are we…
What…

…

CHAPTER TWENTY-SIX

Romeo

MY STOMACH drops out from beneath me. Am I on a roller coaster? No, I'm spinning. Metal crunches, glass breaks. I hold onto Juliet as hard as I can. Pain explodes up my arm, something hits the side of my head, my body is being flung. A weight hits my chest, a scream echoes in my ear.

Juliet.

Where is Juliet?

My brain is telling me to get up, to move, to find her, but nothing happens. It's so dark, I can't see anything.

Someone is crying. Gut-wrenching, full-body sobbing.

My throat is raw, my chest burns.

It's so dark, I can't see.

The crying doesn't stop.

I can't breathe.

Footsteps hurry towards me. Please make them stop crying, please, I can't take it. It hurts me, the crying is hurting me. It's making everything ache.

"Shhhh, shhh, honey. It's okay. You're okay." The shushing keeps going but the crying doesn't stop. "Honey, you gotta take a breath. Blow it out now, blow it out."

Blow what out? There's nothing to blow out, air keeps going in and I can't get it out again. It hurts. I hurt. The crying won't stop. I can't stop.

I can't stop crying.

I can't make it stop.

"Blow it out, blow it out honey. I don't want to sedate you again, come on, breathe with me baby."

It's so dark.

Juliet.

Where's Juliet?

Something taps my cheek, startling me into a gasp. The gasp becomes a cough and pain explodes across my body and I can't help crying out.

"Oh baby, I'm sorry, I bet that hurt. It's okay, you're okay. I got you." I don't know this voice, but she sounds nice. It's not my mom. My mom never says nice things.

Blinking, I can't focus but I want to know who the nice voice is. Someone is leaning over me, fiddling with something above my head. I open my mouth to speak but nothing comes out except another sob.

That was me. I was the one crying.

I can't stop it, can't stop the hiccuping that comes with it, even though each jerk of my lungs sends pain shooting through my chest and back.

The nice voice leans down and strokes my head. "It's okay, honey. The anesthesia does that to some people when they come out of it. Breathe in through your nose and out through your mouth, nice and slow."

I try a few times but the hiccuping throws me off. I can't focus, my brain slips and slides away from me. What am I doing here? Why am I trying to calm down?

Juliet.

Where's Juliet?

I have to find Juliet—the only thing I know for sure.

There's a touch on my cheek again. "Hey there lover boy, focus for me. You gotta calm down before I answer. Breathe in with me. One, two, three, four, five. Now blow it out, two, three, four, five, six." I follow her voice, breathing in slowly and out again between my lips.

Air seeps in through my nose, cold and sharp. I blink again and the face hovering above me comes into focus. Dark brown hair pulled back into a bun. Round cheeks. Brown eyes with crow's feet at the corners. She looks like someone's mom. A nice mom, not like mine. Her face is soft, tired, and worried.

"Blow it out, honey." Her pink lips purse and soft warm breath dances across my forehead. I mimic her, the cold air in my lungs coming out wet and warm, but I don't cough. A hiccup catches me at the end and I moan from the pain. She shushes me, stroking my cheek while I fight not to move.

I copy her breathing a few more times, ignoring everything else except her face until my breathing evens out and the panic subsides. "You're okay," she says over and over again.

Am I?

When I'm calmer, only the occasional jerky breath gives me away, she pulls a stool up to the side of the bed.

I'm in a bed?

"Okay honey, let's chat for a second." I nod, glancing around the room. I'm in a hospital room, a curtain drawn around my bed blocking the noises around me.

"Where's Juliet?" My question is more of a croak, but the nurse nods as if she understood.

"The girl they found with you? She's in surgery now." She's pushing me back into the bed before I realize I'm trying to move. I want to fight her but there's no strength in my body. "Nope, you're staying here young man. You're both in bad shape."

I sink back into the bed, feeling how heavy and hot my right arm is for the first time. "What happened?"

The sinking feeling only gets worse as the nurse tells me what she knows. Juliet and I were picked up by an ambulance on the side of the highway a couple of hours ago. A car coming in the opposite direction had hit us almost head on. As she's talking, memories of the bright lights heading straight at us surface. I'd tried to get out of the way, but there was nowhere to go on the narrow section of road.

"I remember spinning and a crunch, and then nothing." According to the police officer who responded to the scene, my Jeep rolled multiple times while the other car spun out and slammed into a tree on their side of the highway.

While she's talking I try to get a sense of my body. Now that I can focus, there's a cast of some kind on my right arm, my ribs and chest hurt and the left side of my head and face is hot and tight.

"What's your name, honey? Is there someone we can call for you? The ambulance drivers were calling you Romeo but I thought they were just being cute. You keep asking for Juliet, is that her real name?"

I try to smile but my face hurts too much. "Yeah. That's really our names." I grimace. Holding thoughts together is hard. My mind wants to wander, wants to slide back into nothing, even though I desperately want to know what's going on. "Romeo Montgomery and Juliet Caplan."

The nurse just shakes her head. "Who would have thought?"

"Is she going to be okay?" I fight the panic rising in me. My thoughts are so scattered, I can't keep track of what the nurse has told me or what I've told her. My brain is slippery—thoughts start but don't finish.

"I'll be back to check on you later." She starts to walk away but I jerk my left arm, trying to stop her.

"Juliet?"

"If anything happens, I promise to let you know."

She leaves me in the dark and I sink down into oblivion.

CHAPTER TWENTY-SEVEN

Juliet

OMEONE IS crying.

Is it me?

I *was* crying earlier. Why was I crying?

Or was I laughing?

I don't think so.

Maybe?

I take stock of my body. I'm lying down. My toes are there, twitching against the sheet draped over me. An extra vigorous wiggle sends sharp pain up my leg so I stop. Instead of trying to move again, I take a cautious breath, but air is already flowing up my nose, cool and crisp. Something tickles the inside of my nose and my cheek.

Opening my eyes feels like too much work so I keep them closed.

The crying doesn't stop but it sounds farther away.

Fingers. Fingers might be easier to move.

I try one hand, feeling nothing but scratchy sheets beneath my fingers, but no pain. That's a good sign.

I try the other and discover there's another hand holding mine. A gasp and a cry are too loud. They hurt. I want to pull away but there's nowhere to go.

"She's waking up. She's waking up, get the doctor." I know that voice. Mom. Dad.

No.

I don't want them.

Why don't I want them?

Romeo.

Where is Romeo?

I try to ask but all I can do is make a rough noise.

Do I try to open my eyes? It's so hard though.

"Juliet? Baby? Juliet, wake up. Please wake up." Mom is crying. I don't want Mom to cry.

I crack one eye open—everything is white. I pull more of the cool air into my lungs and try again.

Mom's tear-stained face is hovering on my left, her grip on my hand tight. "Hey, hey, it's okay. You're going to be okay." She's whispering over and over.

"Romeo?" I manage to get the word out. Mom's face shuts down at the word. Panic explodes inside my chest at her expression. "What happened? Is he okay? Where is he? WHAT DID YOU DO? WHERE IS HE? ROMEO!"

I pull away from her, even as hands reach for me, pushing at me, pulling at me. The pain in my heart and the pain in my body mingle. All I am is pain. Everything is pain, heart breaking, head pounding, leg throbbing, agony. I'm crying, screaming, sobbing.

Voices are raised above me, there's shouting and crying until a woman's voice carries above them all.

"Get them out of here. That's enough."

The shouting fades away but I don't. I want to. I want to fade away into nothing. If my Romeo, my Troublemaker, isn't here, if they've done something to him, I'll die. I don't want to be here if he's not.

"Sweetheart, don't say that." I was saying it out loud? "You don't really want to die." A kind voice whispers in my ear. "He's alive." My breath catches. Romeo's alive? "He's right next door, honey."

A painful squeeze in my chest reminds me to exhale. "He's okay?"

A gentle hand strokes my cheek. "He's okay. I promise. You get some sleep now."

"I don't want to sleep. I want Romeo." I whisper the words into the dark. When did my eyes close?

"Oh baby, he wants you too, but you're both all kinds of banged up. You can see him after you rest."

I don't want to sleep, I don't want to be in the dark again.

I need him.

CHAPTER TWENTY-EIGHT

Romeo

I HAVE TO get to Juliet. The thought pulls me awake, over and over. I have to find her, make sure she's okay. Beg her to forgive me. How could I have done this to her?

I shift in the bed, uncomfortable, sore, and too tired to move. No. I have to find her. I *will* find her.

It's dark outside. There's just a small light on in the corner of my room, even though the bright light of the hallway seeps in under my door. I roll onto my left side, the weight of the cast on my right arm pressing painfully into my ribs. I tuck my legs up and use them and my good arm to push myself slowly upright until I'm sitting on the side of the bed.

If I wasn't on a mission I'd be embarrassed about the hospital gown I'm sporting, especially since that's all I'm wearing, but I push the thought away.

Juliet. I have to find her.

Gingerly, I put my feet on the floor. Just that action has my head swimming. I close my eyes and take a deep breath, letting the feeling pass. Once it does, I keep pushing until I'm standing. The linoleum floor beneath my bare feet is cold, the sharp smell of astringent clearing some of the fog from my brain. But when I try to stand up straight, a sharp pain exploding through my ribs stops me.

A vague recollection of someone saying "broken ribs" filters through my thoughts. I cradle my arm in its cast against my chest, hunching over it to support the unfamiliar weight and keep the pain from my ribs at bay. The left side of my face feels all wrong, my eye doesn't open all the way and even my teeth feel strange in my mouth.

I need to find Juliet.

Two shuffling steps forward and a tug on my left arm nearly sends me crashing to the ground. The IV snaking from my arm to a bag hung on the side of the bed is stretched tight, same with the thing clipped on the end of my finger. Annoyed, I pull the clip off, but there's still more things attached to me. I start ripping them off, one by one, gritting my teeth against the pain of ripping hair off my chest and arm.

Constant, steady beeps I hadn't registered change to high-pitched alarms and a commotion outside my room moves closer. I've only managed to take a few more slow, unsteady steps before my door swings open.

"Oh honey, no." The nurse from earlier is at my side, hands on my biceps to steer me back to the bed. "I know you want to see her, but she's okay. You're too banged up right now. You need to get back into bed."

I push against her, resisting the pressure turning me away from Juliet. My eyes are locked on the open door, I need to get there. "She needs me. I have to tell her I'm sorry. Please." I force myself to look at the nurse. Her brown eyes are sad, but deter-mined to steer me back to the bed.

"Please. Please. I have to tell. I have to tell her I'm sorry. I'm so sorry. Please let me." I'm begging, pushing against her, my throat raw again from begging.

The nurse just keeps telling me Juliet's fine, I'm fine, that I need to get back in the bed. She won't let me past. How is she so strong? My bare feet slip on the floor.

"Honey, you can't see her right now. She's sleeping. You should be sleeping too. Come on, let's get you back in bed." Her tone is more forceful, I'm making her mad, just like I make everyone mad. Pain keeps catching me around the ribs, in my arm. My face hurts. I make everyone mad all the time. Romeo just pisses everyone off. It's what I do best.

Make my mom mad? Do it all the time. Make my dad mad? I do that just by existing. I can't make Juliet mad. I don't know what I'll do if I do something to make her hate me.

She should hate me.

Look at what I've done.

I have to apologize.

I can't lose her.

"Honey, no one's mad at you, you're not going to lose her. But if you don't get back in that bed, I will call security and sedate you again."

Did the door get closer? I keep pushing, keep trying to get to the door. I wriggle my way out of the nurse's grip and make a dash for it.

The hallway is too bright, it hurts my face, hurts my brain. People in scrubs are moving towards me, but I have to see her. "Juliet?" I glance up and down the hall, where is she?

I'm wheezing, each breath painful. My face is wet. Why is my face wet? I'm crying again. The sound of my sobbing is louder out here, I didn't hear it over the alarms and beeps in my room.

A hand latches onto my bicep before I can pick a direction to look. A different woman in scrubs, this one smaller, younger, her brown hair pulled back in a ponytail, is holding me still. "Stop, you're hurting yourself."

"Juliet. I need to find her."

My nurse comes into view, blocking me from escape. "Listen, if I let you go see that she's okay, will you stop fighting me and get back into bed?"

My heart is screaming at me to say no, to keep fighting until they let me stay with her, but I'm so tired. So, so tired. Sagging on my feet, I nod. "Please, just let me see her."

A wheelchair appears next to me, the new nurse lets go of my bicep and grabs it. "Do you promise to behave?"

I sink into the chair, not hiding how relieved I am to be off my feet. I'm so tired. But I need her. I can't breathe without her.

"I promise." My mumbled words are barely audible but the nurses nod.

Turns out Juliet is closer than I thought, only two doors down from me. Stretched out in the bed, one leg an enormous lump. That's really all I can see from the door, the rest of her is blocked by her father, hunched over the bed, asleep.

My nurse leaves me by the door and tiptoes in, bending down to speak quietly to him. He jerks up, almost headbutting her, snapping his head in my direction. For a second, I can see Juliet on the bed, then he's stalking towards me, face pulled in an angry grimace.

I can't move, can't get out of his way. I pull back, bracing myself for the punch to the face I deserve. Instead, a finger threatens to poke me and a pair of blue-gray eyes just like Juliet's level with mine.

"You did this. She's hurt and it's all your fault." His cold voice is laced with venom. "I knew this would happen. You and your family should have been run out of town years ago." He's right. I'm worse than useless. I'm poison. All I do is hurt people, make them mad. "Look at what you've done." The finger moves to point to my Angel, lying in the bed, fast asleep. Or unconscious, I don't know.

My heart shatters, the pain of my ribs nothing compared to it. "I know, I know. I'm so sorry. I wanted to tell her I'm…"

"You think I would let you anywhere near her again after this?"

I try to take a breath, but can't get past the lump in my throat.

"You will never get to speak to her or see her again. I'll make sure of it."

"Sir," a soothing voice is saying from above my head. "Sir, now is not the time."

Those gray eyes finally look away, setting me free. I stare past him at my Juliet. The only good thing I ever did, and I ruined it. Just like I ruin everything. There's arguing above my head, but I ignore it, knowing I deserve every harsh word he said.

Her chest rises and falls, the heart monitor pumping out a steady beat. I've seen enough.

I lift my hand to tap against the nurse. "It's okay. I'll go now. He's right, I don't deserve to be here."

I can leave now, she's with her family. They don't want me. She doesn't need me. No one needs me now.

CHAPTER TWENTY-NINE

Juliet

MY DREAMS are a swirl of running, laughing, darkness, crying, bright lights and moments of pure bliss that slip away before I can remember them. Something pulls me close to the surface every so often, a voice, someone moving me, but I stay down in the depths of my dreams. I don't want to be awake, not if it means I have to be alone.

"Jules?" Rosie's whisper sinks through the depths of my dream to reach me. "Hey babe. You scared me so bad. What happened? No one will tell me."

My dream was so warm, dark, and empty. Better than the pain waiting for me now I'm awake. I don't answer Rosie, but I scrunch my face.

"Are you awake in there?" There's a long pause, someone is speaking farther away but I can't make out the words. "I won't leave," Rosie answers them. There's another pause then she speaks a little louder near my ear. "Everyone's gone to get food. Come on Jules, wake up. Please?"

"Don't want to," I croak, abandoning the safety of my dark dreams and blinking against the fluorescent lights above me.

Rosie snorts weirdly and I try to focus on her face. She's crying and smiling down at me, wiping tears away with the back of her free hand. "Oh my god, Jules…" She can't finish the words, just puts her head down on the bed beside me and cries. I try to stroke the back of her head with my free arm, but there's so many things sticking in it and attached to it that I give up, settling on squeezing her hand.

We stay like that for a minute before Rosie takes a deep breath and straightens up. "I'm okay now."

I hesitate to answer, mentally assessing my body. "I think I'm kind of okay. I honestly have no idea."

We both explode into wet, snotty giggles. "Jules, I was so scared. No one knew what happened to you guys. And then when the police called…" She shudders and bites her lips. "I don't ever want to go through that again."

"I'm sorry you were so scared. I was pretty scared too." I stare at the ceiling, the same tidal wave of emotion from the restaurant washing through me. The fear, the desperation, the determination. "Where's Romeo? Is he really okay?"

Rosie gives me a watery smile. "He's just a few doors down. He's almost as banged up as you, but he's okay."

I've read thousands of books, but none of them could accurately describe the heart-stopping moment as my brain registered Rosie's words. The utter relief that flooded every part of my body—bubbling through my veins like sparkling water, little bursts of joy popping beneath my skin.

Rosie glances back over her shoulder but there's no one here except us. "The nurse told me he tried to come see you earlier but your dad wouldn't let him. And no one will let me see him."

"His parents won't let you in?" My leg aches, but it hurts even more when I try to shift it, so I stop fidgeting. I'm uncomfortable, but not in pain. It feels as though there's a thin bubble between me and everything else, keeping me safe and keeping everything else just a little bit away from me.

"I feel like an air hockey table," I blurt out. "Wait, that's not important. Why won't they let you see him? Will they let me see him? I want to see him." I'm babbling but my thoughts are scattered, like that air cushion is seeping into my brain and keeping all my thoughts apart, making it hard to focus.

Rosie giggles. "Um, you are high as a kite, Jules."

Her giggles are contagious and I join in, both of us giggling until we cry. And then, like someone flipped a switch, my giggles turn into sobs and the fuzzy safety of my haze crumbles.

"Rosie, why can't I see him?" I try to keep my voice down but it's impossible.

Rosie points at my legs. "Giant cast—don't think they'll let you walk down the hall in that."

"But why can't *you* go see him?"

"The parentals won't let me near his room." Rosie rests her head on my stomach, one of the few places on my body that isn't banged up.

I bite my lip and suck air into my nose so I don't cry. "I thought maybe it was his parents who wouldn't let you go see him."

"I don't think they're here." Rosie's whisper splinters my heart for Romeo. "I've only seen nurses and doctors going into his room."

"But—"

I'm interrupted by the entrance of a nurse in bright blue scrubs. Her soft, round face is kind, her hair pulled back in a tight bun. "Well, look who's finally surfaced. How are you feeling, honey?" She gently pushes Rosie aside so she can look at all the various things attached to me. "Did your folks all go get food?" she asks, inspecting the IV bag on a hook by my head.

Rosie nods. "Yeah, they all went down the street."

The nurse looks thoughtful for a moment. "It'll be a few minutes before I finish up here. If you wanted to *take a stroll* down the hall, now would be a good time." It takes a second for Rosie and I to get what she's hinting at, but realization dawns on our faces at the same time.

"Go!" I flap my hands towards the door at the same moment she turns on her heel.

"I'll be back in a bit," she calls over her shoulder as the door closes behind her.

I sink back into the bed, tears threatening yet again. It's a good thing I'm hooked up to an IV or I'd be dehydrated from all this crying. "Is he okay, really?"

The nurse hums while she writes something down on a tablet. "You know, I thought it was the EMT's being funny when they brought you two in calling you Romeo and Juliet instead of John and Jane Doe, but they were right, weren't they?"

"I don't understand? Those are our names." I think she's trying to make a point but my fuzzy brain isn't cooperating.

She pauses in taking my temperature to pat my arm. "Oh sweetie. Do you know, neither of you has asked about your own selves once? He only wants to know if you're okay, and you keep asking if he's okay. Do you even want to know what your own injuries are?"

I shrug. "My own injuries aren't important if he's not okay."

"He said pretty much the exact same thing." She eyes me. "You two really love each other, don't you?" At my nod, she turns solemn. "You know, he probably saved your life. If he hadn't been holding onto you as tightly as he was, you could have suffered severe head trauma. You still have a pretty major concussion, but it could have been so much worse. The pins in your legs are probably the worst of it—lucky for you the orthopaedic surgeon on call is one of our best."

She stays with me a little while longer, chatting and checking my vital signs. I'm not sure if she's asking me random questions to check for brain injury, or if she's stalling to give Rosie more time to visit Romeo. Talking to the nurse has me feeling a little more normal, less like I'm floating a million miles away.

Pushing to her feet with a final pat on my arm, she smiles. "I have to go finish my rounds dear. I'm sure your parents and the doctor will be back in a little bit. I'll send your friend…?"

"Cousin," I supply at her questioning look. "Rosie."

"I'll send Rosie back over when I get to Romeo's room."

I grab her hand before she can leave. "Is there any way I can see him? Please?"

"You're not going anywhere, not with that leg." The nurse looks thoughtful. "I'll see what I can do. Maybe we can bring him here to see you. He's a little more mobile than you at the moment." She chuckles to herself, like she knows something I don't, but before I can ask what it is she's gone and I'm left awake and alone for the first time.

According to the nurse he's okay. But no one has come to see him yet. He's just sitting there, alone. If I know my Romeo, leaving him to sit alone and stew over his thoughts isn't going to be good for him. I just imagine how much he's blaming himself for what happened, how many times he's run through the night to see what he should have done differently.

I wouldn't change a thing.

I wouldn't take back what I said or did, not one single decision.

I choose him over my parents' plans for me.

I love him and I know he loves me. We were meant to be together.

I have no regrets over what happened between when we left the restaurant and when the accident happened. Every blissful, precious moment, when it was just him, me, and the stars—the rest of the world far away.

"That's an interesting smile." Rosie appears in my doorway, smiling, before half-running to my side. 'He's okay, Jules. He's really okay. Probably better now that he's convinced you're okay too."

I grip her hand, relief flooding my chest, making tears gather in my eyes. I have to stop crying all the time. "Has he been alone this whole time? Where are his parents?"

Rosie drops down into the chair next to me. "I guess his dad came by right after they first called and you two were still out, signed all the paperwork and left again. His mom hasn't been, but…" Rosie leans close, glancing at the doorway. "I think his dad won't let her come. Too much temptation here."

My heart breaks all over again for Romeo. Every time I've cracked my eyes someone's been here with me. Even if I didn't acknowledge them, I knew I wasn't alone. He's been all by himself in that room, worried, in pain, probably scared out of his mind. An idea starts forming in my head, but my thoughts are sluggish and I can't see how to make it all work.

Before I can start trying to figure it out with Rosie, my mom's voice drifts down the hallway towards me. With a sigh, I squeeze Rosie's hand again, preparing for the onslaught now that I'm awake. "Could I fake being asleep again?"

"Oh God, please don't do that to me." Rosie shudders. "You owe me now, I went and checked on your boyfriend for you."

"Fine. Don't leave me alone with them."

There's no time for her to answer before my mom waltzes into the room. My mom doesn't slip into a room, ever. She makes an entrance. Even in a hospital, she's perfectly put together. Linen pants miraculously unwrinkled, her short blonde hair smooth and sleek. The only thing different is that her makeup seems to be mostly worn off. Seeing me awake, she drops the bags in her arms and rushes to my side, pushing Rosie out of the way with her hip.

"Baby!" Kissing my cheeks, she settles into the chair at the side of my bed. "I was so worried." My dad clears his throat from the doorway. "*We* were so worried. How are you feeling? How could you do this to us? What can I get you?"

Her fussing hurts as she keeps touching me and I pull away, even though I have nowhere to go. "Mom, stop." Tears prick at my eyes, which of course sets her off as well. "Mom, you're hurting me." She's wrapped her arms around my shoulders and is crying into my neck. I know the accident scared her, but I'm still angry at them. Still raging inside at how they broke Romeo's spirit, my anger doubling over the fact that I'm lying here, stuck with people I don't want to see while Romeo is next door abandoned and alone. Rosie hovers in the corner, Chuck and Cathy blocking the doorway.

"Come dear." My dad pulls at her shoulders so she gives me some space. "That can't be comfortable for either of you." He manages to pull my mom off me before pulling the second chair in the room close and sitting down.

"The doctors think it's going to be another day or two before they release you, I have flights booked for us to go back to Turkey in a week. That should be enough—"

"A week!" Rosie echoes my cry. "But—"

"A week. It's obvious we can't leave you here again."

I cross my arms, gingerly because of the IV. "No."

Dad levels me with a glare. "This is not up for debate. You are coming home with us, end of discussion. It's obvious we can't trust you to stay here."

Chuck pushes through the door, bristling. "Well now David, let's just remember whose fault this is."

Dad pinches his nose, eyes scrunched. "I'm well aware, Chuck. But no matter where we place the blame, Juliet is still coming back to Turkey with us. The more space we put between them, the better."

Again, everyone is discussing my life as if I'm not here. "I said—I'm not going." No one hears me, too busy discussing it themselves. My mom and Cathy are busy discussing logistics of packing and laundry, my dad and Chuck are talking over flight times and airport rides. Rosie is nowhere to be seen.

"I'm not going." I say louder. Mom pats my hand absently. "I'm staying here." Again, they all ignore me. "Why don't I get to have any say?" I raise my voice, but no one is listening to me. "Mom." She ignores me. "Dad." He glances my way but doesn't answer.

All my life, I've been seen and not heard. Just a decoration for my parents' lives, a trophy to show that they're successful adults with a pretty, submissive, daughter who they'll marry off to their advantage. I'm tired of it, tired of them. I want to be the main character in my own life, not a side character in someone else's.

"I'm not going back with you," I yell, setting free the anger that's been simmering in my gut. "I don't care what you think or what you want. I'm staying here. I'll go live with Melody or Nikki or anybody else if you won't let me stay with Uncle Chuck and Aunt Cathy. But I'm *staying here*!"

I tap the nurse call button on the side of my bed as I finish yelling, although I'm sure they heard me through the open door.

"Now sweetie—" Mom tries to soothe me but I won't be steamrolled this time.

"No. I want you guys to go. Get out of my room." A 'please' is hovering on the tip of my tongue but I bite it off, not wanting to be nice. I don't want to be meek, I want to be bold.

"Everything okay in here, honey?" My favorite nurse comes through the door.

"I want them to leave." My heart is racing in my ears, my face hot and swollen. Tears are threatening but I hold them back. If I cry my parents will see it as weakness.

"Sweetie—" Aunt Cathy tries, but I want to listen to her even less than my own mother.

I close my eyes and lean back against the pillow, exhausted. "I'm not talking about leaving. I'm staying in Oak Hills. And not just because of Romeo. I finally have friends here. I have a life. I want to go to school, normal school. I want to know what it's like to live a normal life."

Someone is leaning over me. I crack one eye open to find the nurse fussing with my monitors. She winks down at me. "Folks, I need to take Juliet's vitals and check on a few things. Visiting hours are going to be over by the time I'm done so y'all might as well go on home now."

Mom huffs. "We don't have to leave for visiting hours, she's a minor."

"Ma'am, she's seventeen and has asked you to leave so she can rest. How about you go wait in the lobby? She'll be just fine on her own tonight. Mostly sleeping and whining at whoever comes to wake her up in the middle of the night to take her vitals. Go home and sleep in your own beds."

I could kiss her for that speech. I just want them to leave so I can think.

There's some more huffing and puffing from my mom and Cathy, but they do it while gathering up their cardigans and purses so I assume they'll leave eventually. The nurse doesn't leave, just stands guard by my bed, acting as a barrier between me and them. Forget Anne Shirley, she's my new hero.

Rosie hasn't reappeared. I catch the nurse's scrubs between my fingers and tug. She turns to me, curious, and leans down when I indicate she should come close. "Is my cousin with Romeo? Don't let them catch her over there, please?"

"We got you kids. Don't worry," she whispers back, patting my shoulder.

Mom bustles over, her arms full of bags. "I was going to give you this later, but here are some pajamas if you want them, and some toiletries." She pauses, setting the bags down on one of the visitor chairs. "I'm so glad you're okay, baby. I was so scared. We'll be back in the morning okay?"

I relent and reach up to give her a hug. "I'm still mad at you, but thank you."

She squeezes gently before pulling away and heading towards the door. Rosie is there waiting for her, a paper cup in her hand. My view is blocked when Dad comes over, chest still puffed.

"Listen, I expect the very best care for my daughter. And if I hear that you let that hoodlum, who got her here in the first place, anywhere near this room, I will personally see to it that you are not only fired but stripped of your license and run out of town. Is that understood? He's not to come in this room."

"Dad," I interrupt his tirade with a tug on his arm. "Leave her alone."

He looks down at me, his eyes still hard. "Our conversation is nowhere near done, young lady. I forbid you to have anything to do with that trash, is that understood?"

The anger I'd tamped down boils back up, but the nurse steps between us before either can explode. "Okay folks, time to let Juliet here get some sleep. I'm sure we'll see you again in the morning."

There's a moment where it looks like Dad might protest, but Mom grabs him by the elbow and pulls him out the door, Chuck and Cathy already waiting in the hall. Rosie ducks past them to run to my side. "Here," she whispers in my ear, leaning down to hug me and slipping something into the bed with me. "He's okay, really. Love you babe, see you tomorrow."

I watch them go, the nurse herding them out the door, dying to see what Rosie slipped in the bed with me.

Something buzzes against my side and it dawns on me. Her phone. Rosie left me her phone. I could kiss her, especially when I see who's trying to video call me.

CHAPTER THIRTY

Romeo

"OH MY God, you look even more awful than you did ten minutes ago."

Rosie's voice echoes through my quiet room, interrupting the constant beeps of the monitors and the quiet murmur of Wheel of Fortune. "Thanks. You look like shit too," I fire back. "Back already? Miss me that much?" Cracking jokes takes so much effort, but it's better than sitting here in the dark.

She closes the door behind her carefully, glancing back into the hallway as she does. As soon as it clicks shut she hurries to the side of my bed. "Our parents are all over there arguing with her about going back to Turkey."

"I knew it." Defeated, I slump back into my pillow. "I knew this would happen. They'll never let her stay, never let her be with me." Everything I suspected would happen is coming true.

Rosie grabs my good hand. "Hey, stop that. You should hear the fight she's putting up. This isn't their decision to make for her, idiot. She's refusing to go. Said she'll go live with Marcus and Melody or Nikki, or anybody that will let her, rather than leave. She wants to stay, dumbass. She wants to stay with *you*."

The hope that inflated my chest at the idea of Jules fighting to stay with me pops when reality crashes in. "Rosie, she can't give up everything for me. What do I have to give her? We're still in high school and my parents hate her just as much as hers hate me. We'll both be disowned and then what?"

I can't let her give up everything for me. I'm not worth it. How many times have I heard Dad tell me that? Tell me how worthless I am any time I screw up—that I'll never amount to anything and end up just like my mom. An empty shell of a person, floating through life from one high to the next.

But God, I want her. I need her. I crave her light, her sweetness. "She's everything. Everything I'm not and better. I need her, but I'll ruin her. I can't do that to her. She's better off without me."

A slap to the face cuts me off. "Do not say that. That's not true and deep down I think you know it, idiot." Rosie's hand hovers near my cheek, ready to slap me again.

"But—"

I'm met with a fierce glare. "Don't 'but' me. She's better with you too. You make her brave, give her something to fight for. If it wasn't for you she'd still be the meek little lamb I always knew. She never stood up for herself or did anything without her parent's permission before you."

"Isn't that a good thing?" I don't understand how Juliet defying her parent's wishes can be an improvement. "I almost got us killed last night." I can't help the waver in my voice as I finally say the words out loud. I almost killed her.

"Can I say something?" We both turn at the new voice in the room. Neither of us noticed the door opening and closing, but the younger nurse who helped me check on Juliet is standing there. "You probably saved her life, actually. If her head had hit the dashboard at full force, I don't think she'd be here now. That cast on your arm is proof that you held on tight and stopped her from doing exactly that." She comes further into the room, still talking even as she reads the monitors and makes notes. "We call them car accidents for a reason, you know. You didn't do it on purpose."

"Yeah, but if we hadn't been running away—"

This time it's Rosie who interrupts me. "Bozo, you guys only ran away because our parents are being unreasonable."

I mull their words over while the nurse takes my blood pressure, the band squeezing my biceps hard enough to make me feel a little sick. My head is pounding again and my arm is hot and aching. Even my face hurts.

"How's your pain?" The nurse asks, reading my mind.

"No. No painkillers. I don't want them."

"Oh sweetheart, don't try to be a martyr. Being in pain isn't helping you think straight."

Rosie looks at me for a long second, before clearing her throat. "His mom, uh...has had issues."

Understanding dawns across the nurse's face. She looks over the tablet in her hand. "How about I see if the doctor can prescribe you some non-narcotics?"

I squeeze my eyes closed and nod. "That would be okay, I guess."

There's shouting in the hallway outside and we freeze, listening, but I can't make out the words.

Leaning down to give me an awkward hug, Rosie kisses my cheek. "I better go, that sounds like my dad." She straightens and starts to walk away before turning back. "Hey, did your phone survive? Juliet's got smashed."

"His belongings are probably in that bag there." The nurse points to the bottom of my bed. Rosie rummages around in it and pulls out my phone, miraculously intact, apart from the long crack down the front of the screen.

"Keep this on you, okay? I'll give Jules my phone so you guys can at least text or something." She squints her eyes and looks at me again. "Um, maybe don't Facetime her. Just to be safe."

"That's not a promise I can make." My fingers are already fumbling at the screen.

"How about we keep the lights turned down? So you don't scare your girlfriend." The nurse chimes in. Do I look that bad?

Chuckling, Rosie disappears out the door, leaving me staring at the ceiling, my brain a whirl of anxiety and slippery thoughts. "Do you really think I saved her, or are you just telling me that so I don't cause a scene?" I clutch my phone in my good hand, too scared of what I'll find on it to unlock it. It's probably dead anyway.

I know there's messages from my friends, Rosie said they'd been looking for us for hours after we left the restaurant. "Hey," I ask the nurse, a question occurring to me for the first time. "How long have we been here?"

She does some quick counting while I run a finger up and down the crack on my phone's screen. Somehow, knowing it could be sharp but isn't cutting me, calms my need to do *something*. "It's been about twenty-four hours, give or take. You were both out for a while."

My phone is definitely dead. "I don't suppose you guys have phone chargers around here?"

The nurse nods towards the counter on one end of the room, wrapping up whatever it is she's doing. "Your friend left one here for you." God, I love Rosie. The nurse brings it over and plugs it in for me, connecting my phone so it can charge. "I need to go see my next patient, but call if you need anything."

"Can I see her?"

She shakes her head. "Legally, I can't let you into her room, not after her father expressly forbade you from entering." She pauses, probably because she can see the disappointment written on my face. "But I can suggest you go check out the chapel on this floor. It's usually pretty quiet—not a lot of people go in there."

She leaves me in the dark, confused. The chapel? Why would she suggest I go to the chapel?

Staring at the ceiling doesn't yield any answers. Instead, I just keep going over what I remember from the accident. And from what happened before.

It's all jumbled up and hazy in my mind—staring at my beautiful Angel across the table, the plummeting of my stomach as her parents surprised us there. My heart leaping when she came to my defense, even knowing that every word her father and uncle said about me and my family was true. The pain in my chest as I walked away from her, thinking I was doing the right thing. How my world went from pitch black to rainbow hued the second she put her hand in mine and told me to run, her blinding smile all I could see.

And that doesn't even begin to express the bliss of that private, perfect hour we spent tucked away in the dark. With nowhere to go, we'd parked in an empty field, gazing at the stars and avoiding making plans. Touching her, holding her, tasting the skin of her neck and shoulders while we laughed and discovered each other all over again in the back seat of my Jeep. That stolen hour cementing my need to do anything and everything in my power to keep her. That I couldn't live without her now that I knew what it was to have Juliet. I'd tasted the forbidden fruit and couldn't live without it again.

And she's right there. So close.

My thumb rubs the crack on my screen while I wait for it to charge. I can't put it off any longer, so I hit the power button, the screen blinding in the dark of my room. After a few seconds the notifications start pouring in, but I ignore them. There's nothing there that can't wait. Instead, I open my contacts and look for Rosie's name to start a video chat with Juliet. I won't be able to think about anything else until I see her and talk to her.

"Hi! Hey, oh my gosh, let me look at you. Are you okay? I love you." The flood of questions and reassurances start the second she answers "Everyone keeps saying that you're okay, but no one will tell me how you actually are. I've been so scared. Where are you hurt? I love you. I love you. They want to make me go back to Turkey, but I—"

"Angel?" I interrupt, a smile stealing across my face even though it pulls on the stitches on my left cheek. "Hey, I'm okay. Really. Are you okay?"

She takes a breath, smiling back. "Yeah. I'm okay. Mostly."

"I love you. I'm so sorry about what happened." I have to say it.

Her smile turns relieved. "I love you too, so much. Right, I need to know exactly how you are. Please. You have some…" She points to her own cheek.

"I have some cuts on my face, the one up by my eyebrow needed stitches, but the rest are not too bad." I hold up the phone with my good arm so she can see my cast. "Broke my right arm and a couple of ribs too. What about you? I know you broke your leg, but what else?"

"How did you know I broke my leg?" She flips her camera so I can see the uneven lumps in her bed, one regular sized leg and one twice the size.

"They didn't tell you? I hulked my way out of here last night and snuck over to see you. Your dad wouldn't let me in the room, but I saw the cast."

Juliet giggles and the sound relieves a tightness in my chest I didn't even know was there. That magical, musical sound that I was terrified to never hear again.

"No, they didn't tell me. I have a concussion, some big bruises and I'm sore all over. They're keeping me in for observation for now, because of the concussion and the surgery on my leg. Did you hear they put pins in it? I'm bionic now."

She fills me in some more on how she's feeling. I'm listening, but I'm so relieved to see she's okay and doesn't hate me for what happened, that I don't retain any of it.

"I wish I could come see you." I interrupt her.

"Why can't you? I'm the one with the broken leg." Her teasing question is another patch to my broken heart.

"Your dad specifically banned me from your room and the nurses can't break the rules." I shift, attempting to get comfortable, eventually laying my bandaged arm across my stomach and resting the phone against it. "My nurse suggested I go to the chapel if I wanted to get out of my room, but I don't—"

"Mom wanted to wheel me over there earlier but I refused. I don't want to go to church. Geez, that's been one of the nicest things about being here this summer—not having to spend all Sunday at church with my parents."

My brain is still moving slowly, but something about the nurse's suggestion worms its way through my fuzzy thoughts. "Hang on Angel. Do you think the nurses would be willing to wheel you over there?"

"Yeah, my nurse said she would but why—"

"Your dad can't stop me from visiting the *chapel*."

"Ohhhhhh." She drops the phone, knocking it into the side of the bed as she hunts for something. "Sorry!" Her voice echoes above the screen somewhere. "I got excited. Hang on…" There's a whirl of lights and ceiling and then her face is on the screen again, grinning. "How's your Hail Mary?"

CHAPTER THIRTY-ONE

Juliet

SOFT LIGHT shines from sconces in the wall, their glow highlighting Romeo's black eye. He's turned sideways in the front pew of the chapel, waiting for me. Cool air blows from the vents, dancing over my skin. The pajamas Mom gave me are much more comfortable than a hospital gown, the shorts and tank top perfect for dealing with my unwieldy leg.

"Hey, Beautiful." His smile calms the panic that's been lodged in my heart for hours. Panic that I would be dragged out of here without a chance to see him again.

My nurse parks my wheelchair in front of him. "I'll be back in about twenty minutes." She tiptoes away without waiting for either of us to acknowledge her.

I reach out to take Romeo's good hand, running my finger over his knuckles. "I…" I swallow, fighting the tears that threaten to overwhelm me. I don't want to cry now, not when I don't know when I'll see him again. "Are you really okay?"

"Yeah, Angel. I'm okay. About as okay as you are, I guess." He lifts his good hand to stroke my cheek, his fingers barely touching me.

"I'm not broken."

He just raises an eyebrow at me.

"I mean, my leg is broken, but the rest of me is fine."

"Babe, you're not fine. I almost got us both killed." The sadness and regret in his words slice at me.

"No. You *saved* me." I reach forward to try and touch him but the arm of the wheelchair is in my way. Grunting, I attempt to shift but can't get a good angle. Giving up, I lean downward until my forehead is resting on his chest. I whisper my words into the dark of the chapel, not sure if he can hear me. "You're the first thing I've ever truly wanted to fight for. I'm not giving up on us."

Fingers tangle in my greasy hair and Romeo kisses the top of my head. "Why are you fighting for me? Am I really worth it?"

I sit up so fast the room spins. "Don't say that. Of course you are."

He doesn't respond, just squeezes his eyes shut. But his hand on my neck twitches, his fingers stroking my skin.

Twisting again, this time I manage to prop myself up with my good leg. Reaching out to pull him close, Romeo melts into my arms. His arms reach around my back, his cast heavy against me. For a long moment we stay that way, breathing each other in.

I turn my nose into the side of his neck, breathing in the scent of him. We're both dirty and disgusting, but I don't think either of us cares. I sink into his shoulder, letting him take my weight, needing the reassurance of his body against mine.

"I love you." He whispers, kissing the top of my head again. "I'm so sorry."

I reach up to press my lips to his cheek, careful to avoid the scratches. "I love you too. No more apologies." I lay kisses in a line across his cheek to his lips.

With a quiet moan, he kisses me back, our lips dancing. Romeo is gentle, kissing me delicately, as if I might break again. "I'm not made of glass." I growl, deepening the kiss. Taking a fistful of his hospital gown in each hand, I pull him closer.

For a split second I think he's going to pull away, but then he slides his hands up my back, one burying itself in the hair at the back of my neck. His tongue slips past my lips, tangling with mine. A fire burns low and hot in my belly, demanding more.

"I love you." He pulls back far enough to whisper the words, before diving back in. The arm of the wheelchair digs deep into my stomach, but I ignore it and the ache in my back from the awkward angle.

A need to reassure myself that he's truly whole has my hands sliding over his chest. Relief fills me as his solid torso is firm beneath my fingers. "I was so scared." The thought escapes me. His abs tense under me. "I was so afraid I would never get to see you again. I was scared in the car as we drove away. Scared they'd hurt you deeper than I could fix."

I don't let him answer, stealing his protests away with more kisses. If I could take his worries away and keep him safe from them I would. Maybe the best I can do right now is distract him from the dark corners of his mind.

"Angel…" Romeo pulls away, my name on his lips.

"Shhh." I lean over to kiss my way down his neck and along his jaw. "No talking."

"But…" Without looking, I press my fingers over his lips, cutting off his protests.

"We're alive. Everything else can wait."

After a few minutes, I pull back. Romeo's chocolate eyes are nearly black in the dim lighting. They drink me in and I can't look away. Softly, he lifts one hand to trace it from the top of my head, down my cheek and along my neck.

I tip my head to the side as his fingers slide down my shoulder and along my arm. He touches every inch of my skin, silent. I lift my hand as he traces each finger before his hand drifts back up the underside of my arm and across my collarbone. "I'm here." I whisper as he leans forward to press his lips along the path his fingers took.

"Don't leave me." If the chapel wasn't so silent I wouldn't have heard his hushed words. Tears escape me as they sink into my heart.

I place my hand on the back of his head as his lips trail across my shoulder. "I'm not leaving. No matter what, I'm staying with you."

My finger grips his hair as he kisses along my other arm. The feathery touch tickles but I don't giggle. Eyes closed, I let myself drown in the sensation. "I won't let them take me away." I reassure him.

"I love you."

"I love you."

We whisper over and over to each other until the nurses come to take us back to our rooms.

I don't know how I'm going to save us, but I have to try.

CHAPTER THIRTY-TWO

DAD: I'm going to the store. Try not to break anything while I'm gone.

DAD: I realize typing is difficult but some kind of acknowledgement that you've received my message would be the polite thing to do. Your injuries are no excuse for disrespect.

ROMEO: Got it.

DAD: Watch your tone young man.

ROMEO: Sorry.

BENNY: Are you up for visitors?

MARCUS: Yeah, we're so bored.

ROMEO: Yeh, cAll fo duty ready for actual. ducking cast! fcking mfat finders.

BENNY: This way I stand a chance of beating you for once. We'll be there soon.

MARCUS: Is it cool if Melody comes? I think she wants to go next door and see the girls.

ROMEO: If she cans git though teh door. Lockdown ovre there. Can't git

ROMEO: Duck. fuck. mhate this. Yes. Cool.

MARCUS: Try not to break anything else before we get there. Did your dad find the plate you dropped last night? Wait, tell me when we get there, I can't read another one of your painful texts.

ROMEO: Duck u

Dear Principal St. Clair,

We regret to inform you that our daughter, Juliet Caplan, will not be able to take the enrollment spot you so generously offered her for the upcoming school year. After much consideration, we feel that it is better for her to accompany us overseas to finish her high school education. Please ignore any requests you receive from her, or anyone else, regarding the matter. We will be returning overseas in a few weeks, once she is able to travel more comfortably.

Please thank your son Perry for us, we know he tried his best to befriend her. We believe Juliet has suffered from a little too much freedom while visiting her cousin, which unfortunately resulted in her being rude to Perry. We would be happy to allow him to visit while she is recovering. If he has any friends he would like to invite that can also keep Juliet's cousin, Rosaline, company that would be wonderful. Both girls have been confined to the premises for the time being. We trust your and Perry's judgement in picking an acceptable companion.

Sincerely,
Dr. and Mrs. David Caplan

ROSIE: I will pay $50 to anyone who can slip me a laxative.

MELODY: What do you need it for? Are they feeding you too much fiber?

ROSIE: Ha. Ha.

NIKKI: Actually, that's a really good question. What DO you need it for?

TIA: If you're planning on slipping it in someone's drink, you need the liquid kind.

STEPH: I KNEW IT! That was you wasn't it!!!!!!!!!!!!!!

TIA: I don't know what you're talking about Steph….

ROSIE: I need to get rid of Perry. He dragged Conner over here with him, but I won't torture him. Probably.

NIKKI: Are you guys still grounded over there? It's been a week, aren't they done punishing you yet?

ROSIE: Apparently not? This is the freaking WORST.

TIA: Found some in my bathroom, I'll be there in 5.

TROUBLE: Is the coast clear?

ANGEL: No typos? I'm impressed.

ANGEL: Perry and Conner are still here. I'm hiding in the bathroom. Thank goodness no one expects me to move quickly. Please tell me you aren't going to try to sneak over here? It's too risky.

TROUBLE: Finally getting the hang of typing with my cast on. I have to go slower. Also voice to text is my friend.

TROUBLE: I can't keep watch from the den, my dad is in there on his phone. You'll have to text me when they leave.

ANGEL: Don't do it. He'll see you. It's not worth it.

TROUBLE: I need to see you. Just for a minute.

ANGEL: I want to see you too, but if you get caught, it'll be even worse.

TROUBLE: You know I don't care. I don't want to fight with you about it tonight. Please Jules, I need to see you. It's been two weeks, I'm dying without you.

ANGEL: I know, but if they catch you sneaking over here, you won't be the only one who gets in trouble. They'll have me on a plane to who knows where before the sun rises.

TROUBLE: I hate it when you're right.

CHAPTER THIRTY-THREE

Juliet

I WENT TO the zoo in Budapest with my mom when I was little. There was a leopard in one of the cages that prowled back and forth in front of the viewing window. At the time I'd thought it was so beautiful, the way it showed off for the crowd, pacing back and forth. A second leopard was lounging on top of a hutch behind it, sleeping with one eye open. I'd been disappointed in it, thinking it was sleepy.

Now I'm pretty sure they were both just depressed.

Rosie paces back and forth in front of my window, flipping through TikTok while I lay in bed listening to my third book of the day. We've turned into that pair of captive animals and I don't know how much longer we can stay sane.

We got rid of Perry and Conner an hour ago. I don't know why Conner keeps going along with this plan, but at least he's there for Rosie, which takes away a little bit of my guilt over her being punished along with me. They've had their heads together, planning something, the last few times he and Perry have come over.

I'm sure Rosie abandoning me to Perry's attention is her way of getting back at me for all of this. I can't even be mad. I deserve it.

"What is he doing?" Rosie stops pacing, staring out the window.

"What?" I drag myself out of the fantasy world I'd been lost in at Rosie's words. "Who's doing something?" I struggle to push myself up to sitting in the bed, irritated at the heavy cast on my leg.

"Who do you think?"

I wince at the irritation in her voice, knowing I deserve it. I'm surprised she's still talking to me at this point. "Your lover-boy is calling."

"No he's not." I hold up my new phone, the only thing visible is the audiobook app I was using.

Rosie steps away from the window. "Yes he is. Come here."

She helps me get off the bed, holding my crutches for me until I can work my way to standing. They only let me start using the crutches a few days ago, not trusting me to be safe until I was cleared by the doctor for my head injury. I'm not supposed to be on my phone or watch tv—I'm not even supposed to read. Thank goodness for audiobooks and Rosie convincing Mom I needed a phone.

"What's going on?" I make my way through the dim room to see for myself. Bright light still bothers me. For all my parents want to get me away from Romeo, my mom is too scared of my injuries to force me on a plane yet.

Leaning against the wall, I peek between the blinds at the house across from us. Romeo's doing something in his room, oblivious to the fact that I'm watching. He's hanging something in his window frame and after staring for a second I realize it's a string of lights. He bends down to plug it in and the whole window glows.

Pink and white lights illuminate his window, cutout hearts dotted around and framing him as he stands in the center, waving at me. The lights aren't like the big Christmas ones I'm used to, these are tiny, sparkling, and fairy-like. They're soft enough that they only make my eyes squint a little and don't trigger an instant headache like brighter ones do. He waves the phone clutched in his hand.

"I got it." Rosie moves to grab mine before I can move from my spot. "God, you guys are so gross. Even though I should still be pissed at you for getting me in trouble too, it's really hard to stay mad when he does crap like this." Rosie kisses the top of my head, handing me my phone. "I'll be back in a bit. Don't do anything stupid."

My phone buzzes with a video call the second Rosie puts my phone in my hand. Romeo's face fills my screen. Just that brief glance at the screen has my eyes watering and an ache starting in my head, so I look away after a second. "Hey." My voice is soft in the quiet room. I try to get comfortable, leaning against the window seat, but I can't squeeze in it like I used to. Instead, I perch half on the seat and lean my head against the cool glass, eyes closed.

"Crap, I forgot about the screen thing. Do you want me to hang up and call back?" His voice is filled with worry for me, glancing across to his window. "I'm so sorry Angel. I just wanted to surprise you and see your face. I didn't think—"

"Hey, it's ok." I cut him off with a quiet sigh. "I love the lights and the hearts, they're adorable and sweet. Even if I think you're going to get us both in trouble with it." I pinch the bridge of my nose, eyes still closed against the light. Exhaustion from the day creeps over me. I don't want to take it out on Romeo, it's not his fault.

"Angel, I'm so sorry." His voice is thin and laced with worry. I peek one eye across to his house. He's got his good hand buried in his hair, tugging at it. My fingers flex, wanting to be the ones tugging on the soft strands. His phone is pinched between the fingers of his hand in the cast. We're quite the beat-up pair.

"Romeo…" He's not listening to me, still tugging on his hair and pacing in front of the window. "Hey!" I raise my voice just a hair to get his attention. "It's okay. I'm just tired from this afternoon. Dinner was…an experience."

With my parents still in town, dinner has been a semi-formal affair every night. They also keep inviting Principal St. Clair, meaning Rosie and I have been doing our best to ignore but not insult Perry. Even my broken leg hasn't gotten me out of these dinners. I just get propped on one end of the huge dining table, my leg arranged awkwardly on a low stool, making me even more of the center of attention than I would have been.

The only bearable thing about the dinners is that Rosie has insisted Conner come too. He's turned out to be a pretty decent friend, somehow able to both banter with Perry and roll his eyes at him behind his back. I don't know that I'd trust Conner, he's a born politician and charmer, but at least he can steer the conversation away from Perry's ego every once in a while.

"I should let you go. I'm going crazy over here Angel. My dad keeps working from home, so he's just *always here.* I can't get away from him. Every time I see him, he reminds me that everything is all my fault." I keep my eyes closed, letting him talk. "I know it's my fault. I don't need him to remind me. I just…" He lets out a frustrated grunt, but the despair in his voice worries me. He's not in a good place mentally—it's obvious from our clandestine conversations.

"Hey." I interrupt the inevitable tirade. "Take a breath, okay?" I wait until I hear his exhale. "Stop blaming yourself. It was an accident." I repeat the same thing I tell him every time we've talked. "No one could have known it was going to happen. Isn't your mom there? Can't she help?"

"Mom is…checked out."

My back is hurting from the awkward angle. The weight of my leg pulls at my side uncomfortably. "I'm going to go lay down, okay? Thank you for the surprise, it was just what I needed. Can you give me a second to get sorted out?" Once more, I crack my eyes open to see what Romeo's doing. He's watching me from his window, face pulled in worry and regret. I know he wants to be here, to be able to help me instead of watching me helplessly through the window, but I'm so tired tonight.

Tossing my phone onto my pillow, I grab my crutches and make my way to the bed, trying hard not to think about Romeo watching me through the window. Knowing he's blaming himself for each halting movement. Instead, I focus on moving as smoothly as I can, schooling my face so he doesn't know how much my head is aching.

"Jules…" His pained word floats up as I lower myself to the edge and set my crutches down.

"I'm fine." I keep reassuring him, but it's never enough. He's convinced I'm irreparably damaged. "No more blaming yourself tonight, okay? Just talk to me. Tell me a story or something." The ache in my head is joined by the now familiar ache in my leg. "Actually, hang on. I'm going to take a pain killer now, will you read to me until I fall asleep? I just want to hear your voice."

CHAPTER THIRTY-FOUR

Romeo

JULIET'S BREATH is soft and even through the phone. I stopped reading the book she'd picked out five minutes ago, doing nothing except lay here in the dark, listening to her breathe.

In.

Out.

In.

Out.

Why can't this be the rest of my life? Listening to her breathe. Just listening. No more making decisions, no more fucking it all up. No more ruining everything.

They'll never let me see her again. It doesn't matter what I do. I'm wrong.

Bad.

Tainted.

She can't be mine anymore.

In.

Out.

In.

Out.

Two weeks. Fourteen days. Three hundred and thirty six hours since I've been near her. More if you count the time in the hospital.

The last time I saw her was in the chapel at the hospital. We hadn't talked much, just touched each other, trying to convince ourselves that the other was really truly okay. To cement in our hearts the knowledge that the other was there. That we weren't dreaming, that we'd both made it out of the car accident alive.

I almost wish I hadn't.

My own breath is harsh in the quiet of my bedroom.

In.

Out.

In.

Out.

No. Not almost.

It would have been better for everyone if I hadn't walked away from the accident.

Juliet could have thought of me fondly—as the boy she loved one summer who went out in a blaze of glory.

Our parents would mourn me as a young life cut off too soon. But they'd never have to live with the heartbreak of all the times I'm sure to disappoint them in the future.

My friends would think of me sometimes. Would they miss me? Or would they move on? Marcus would take my place as the "fun one." Benny would stop keeping antacids in his locker. Rosie would tell off Conner or Fritz or Marcus instead of me.

Maybe they'd miss me, but they'd move on.

In.

Out.

In.

Out.

Juliet would move on. She'd find someone else, someone better than me. Someone who could love her without hurting her like I have. Like I would.

I don't want to hang up. Fear that it's the last time I'll ever get to hear her grips my gut, icy tendrils creeping their way up my spine.

I was reading her a book I'd never heard of. *Deerskin* by Robin McKinley. It was dark, darker than I was expecting, but I understood why she wanted this book right now. She told me it was the book she read when she needed to feel things, when she needed something to help her feel sad and angry and cry. We haven't got to the happy ending yet, but so far it's intense, I can feel the main character's pain deep in my own bones.

The last line I'd read, about the main character still breathing because she didn't know how to stop, echoes in my mind.

In.

Out.

In.

Out.

I didn't know how to stop breathing. How to make it stop hurting.

Not just my body.

My soul ached.

My body aches all the fucking time, but I never take the pills they gave me. Hid them in the depths of my gear bag and pretended they didn't exist, even if I thought about them every hour. Recited the dosage on the bottle to myself over and over.

I need to feel the ache. Need to feel the pain.

I deserve to feel the pain. I earned every second of it.

I ruined her in every sense of the word.

Ruined her soul. Ruined her mind. Ruined her body.

I was the devil.

I lay in the dark, counting her breaths and my own. Oxygen seeps into my lungs, unwanted. Her dad is right—I'm trash, just like my mom, just like my dad.

In.

Out.

In.

Out.

"I love you." I whisper into the phone. I should tell her everything while I have the chance. Now, while she can't hear me, because I don't deserve for her to understand what I feel. Because I took what wasn't mine to take. Like my dad said.

"Angel. You're the best thing that I've ever known. I didn't know anything in my life could be as good as you." I stop and suck in a shaky breath. "I thought people were only this perfect in movies, but then there you were. You saw past the kid everyone here knows me as. How do you know everything about me and still want to be near me? Let alone love me?"

There's a rustling noise through the phone and I freeze, terrified she's going to wake up and hear my confession. I lay in the silent darkness of my room, eyes trained on the window across from me. If I stare hard enough, could I see her in the darkness? Could I crawl into the bed with her, feel her in my arms one more time?

"Why do you love me? Why didn't you run away when you should have?" My voice is loud in the quiet of my house. Mom has been passed out for hours and Dad is out—I don't care where. I'm just glad he's finally gone.

In.

Out.

In.

Out.

My breath matches hers.

I breathe in my need for her.

I exhale it. Get rid of the ache for her.

"I love you."

In.

Out.

In.

Out.

"I'm sorry. So. Fucking. Sorry."

In.

Out.

In.

Out.

The bottle shakes in my hand. The promise of relief rattles inside.

In.

Out.

In.

Out.

"Find someone better. Find everything you deserve."

In.

Out.

In.

Out.

A handful of pills fills my palm, spills onto the carpet.

In.

Out.

In.

Out.

"You're the best thing that's ever happened to me, Angel. Don't waste your life on me.

In.

Out.

In.

Out.

My phone slips out of my fingers, thumping to the floor.

In.

Out.

In.

Out.

"I just need it to stop. I'm so tired."

In.

Out.

In.

Out.

I choke on the pills, coughing so hard my broken ribs stab me over and over.

In.

Out.

In.

Out.

"Don't cry for me."

In.

Out.

In.

Out.

I lay in the dark, listening. Someone cries far away, calling my name. Maybe I'm just dreaming it, dreaming that my Angel is calling for me.

Still breathing.

In.

Out.

In.

Out.

In.

Out.

Out.

Out.

…

…

…

CHAPTER THIRTY-FIVE

Juliet

MY HANDS are raw from pounding them against my window. It didn't matter how much I screamed, how loud I yelled, I couldn't escape the prison of my room.

His words to me, "don't cry for me," echo in my head. The sound of pills rattling in a bottle are etched into my dreams, a sound I'll never forget. I screamed for him to stay with me, to stop, talk to me. But he never responded to my crying. I'd woken up my entire house but he never answered.

Instead, I was trapped in my golden tower while Rosie broke into Romeo's house. Helpless as the ambulance came flying down the street. My raw throat doesn't make a difference as he's wheeled out on a stretcher and loaded into the back.

My gasping sobs are the only thing I hear as they drive away.

I'll never forget the horror of realizing what he'd done as my brain struggled to claw its way to consciousness. Screaming his name, I'd thrashed and fallen off the bed, crawling towards my door, cast dragging and catching painfully on the floor, only to find it locked. In my fuzzy-headed state I couldn't get it open so I'd resorted to pounding and yelling until Mom threw it open, Rosie and everyone else right behind her.

It was Rosie who broke into his house and called the paramedics when she found him on the floor, the half-empty pill bottle next to him.

"Shhhhh, shhhhhh." Mom has her arms around me, pulling me back towards my bed. I struggle against her, but I'm too weak to get free. "Go to bed, go to sleep Juliet. There's nothing you can do now."

The pain pill I took earlier drags at me, pulling me towards oblivion. I can't sleep, I have to know he's okay before I can relax. How am I going to know what's happening if I drift off? I don't trust them to tell me the truth.

My eyes are so heavy, fighting to keep them open is so hard. So hard.

The adrenaline coursing through me is fading, leaving me a limp mess. "I need to know..." My voice is rough and talking hurts.

"Rosie is there. Go to sleep. I'll wake you up if there's any news."

"I don't believe you." I don't have the strength to lie to her, to make my words pretty for her.

Mom strokes my head. "I promise. I'm sorry, baby. I'm so sorry. I need you to be safe, okay? I need you to stay with me." She keeps whispering, laying on the bed next to me, my back nestled against her chest. I don't want to sleep, don't want to miss anything but the dark pulls inexorably at me.

"I have to know, Mom." I swim up to the surface long enough to whisper.

She holds me close, rubbing my back. "I know baby, I promise. You'll know. We'll all know. But you have to stay here, you have to stay with me to find out. You can't disappear on me, okay? You can't leave us too."

Sleep washes over me like a tidal wave, impossible to fight. I slip into the darkness, my heart bleeding out, my mind going numb.

I WAKE WITH a start, panic clawing at my throat. "Romeo?" I'm halfway up, but tangled in the sheets. I'm trapped. Again. I have to get to him, I have to get there.

A hand rests on my shoulder, stopping my trashing. "Alive. He's alive."

I freeze before collapsing back onto the bed. "He is?" Now that my eyes are open, I realize it's not Mom on the bed next to me but Aunt Cathy. Instead of curling up against her like I would Mom or Rosie, I scrub my hands over my face.

"Yes, dear. He's alive. They got him to the hospital in time." Aunt Cathy's words are measured.

My hands slide around the bed, searching for my phone. "I need to call him. I need to talk to him."

Aunt Cathy hands me the phone, but doesn't let go when I try to take it from her. "He won't be able to talk to you, sweetheart."

"Why? What's wrong with him?" Panic grips my lungs.

"He's on a seventy-two hour hold. No phone, no contact allowed. He did leave you a note though." Cathy reaches behind her to pull something off my nightstand. "Are you going to be okay if I leave? Your mom didn't want you left alone, but I need to use the restroom."

I take the plain white envelope from her, my name scrawled across the front, and nod. "Go ahead." It would be unkind to say the truth, that I don't want her here while I read whatever letter Romeo left me. I don't want her. I want him.

ANGEL,

You were right. I am trouble with a capital T. Last night…last night was scary. I think I'm a little afraid of myself right now. I bet you're probably scared of me too. You should be.

I want to tell you sorry. I'm sorry I scared you. I'm sorry for crashing into your life and ruining it. I won't say sorry for loving you, because loving you is the one good thing I've done in my stupid life. I'm just sorry that you loving me ruined everything.

I guess I'm not allowed to have my phone or anything so I won't know if you get this letter or not. I'm trusting Rosie to make sure you do. I'm going to try and get my head on straight.

If you don't want anything to do with me after this, I understand. But I want you to know this isn't your fault, this is all me. I'm the one who made the mess and I'm the one who has to clean it up. I don't want you to go back to Europe thinking that I'm still broken. So I'm going to do everything I can to get my mind in a better place so when you leave, you don't have to worry or feel sorry for me.

I love you.

I always will,
ROMEO

I fold up Romeo's letter and slide it back into the envelope. I tuck it under my pillow so no one is tempted to take it from me and pull out my phone. It's time to make a plan.

CHAPTER THIRTY-SIX

Romeo

ROMEO,

I am so mad at you. So, so mad.

I don't know if I'm supposed to say that to you right now, but it's true. How could you doubt me? Did you really think I would let my parents keep us apart? You didn't think I would fight tooth and nail to stay with you?

How could you leave me like that? Don't you know I need you too?

I need you too.

You need you.

Don't you want to know what happens next? You've read books, you know there's always a moment so dark that you think it's the end. And it never is. There's always a way out, always a reason to turn the page and keep reading.

I never told you my least favorite thing about our names.

I hate that Romeo gives up. That he's so quick to throw in the towel. He doesn't fight to stay, to see what could happen next.

You're not allowed to do that to me.

In the play, Juliet had a plan so they could be together. She had it all worked out. If Romeo had just waited five freaking minutes, they would have lived happily ever after. Instead, he gave up and everything ended in tragedy.

We're not going to end in tragedy, Romeo.

That's not our story.

So you listen to me. You're going to get it together. You're going to trust in yourself and when you don't trust yourself, you're going to trust me. You're going to trust that I have faith in you even when you don't trust yourself. And you're going to fake it until you start to believe, like I do.

And if you need more than just my faith in you, you're going to trust Marcus. And Rosie. And Benny. And Nikki. And Fritz. Even Tia, Steph and Conner. If all of us want you around, then it doesn't matter what anyone else says.

You're going to stick around to watch the stars with me again. And see Fritz and get an ice cream headache with me. You have to take me to our senior prom 'cause Rosie and I are going to pick out the most killer dresses ever, and I'm going to be pissed if I don't get to see you in a tux. I want to slow dance with you, then ditch the others to go kiss in a dark corner somewhere and get busted by a chaperone.

Got it?

See you soon,

JULES

I tuck her letter under my pillow and turn to stare at the wall.

I got it.

I don't know if I have the strength to do what Juliet needs me to do, but I'm determined to try.

The voice in my head that tells me I'm not worth the trouble is still loud, still hard to ignore, but I'm fighting it. I'm trying to listen to my Angel's voice that tells me there's still life left to look forward to. That I deserve to experience it.

I pick up the book she sent with her letter. It's a copy of the same book I was reading her that night, *Deerskin*. Now that I've got past that first section, I know why she sent it. Why it makes her feel things.

It makes me feel things.

In the book, the moon gives Lissar the gift of time, time to grow strong, to learn her own strength away from anyone's idea who she is and who she should be. I feel that on a visceral level. Everyone expects me to screw up—to make a mess.

I'm going to get out of here and prove them wrong.

CHAPTER THIRTY-SEVEN

Juliet

"**Y**OU CAN either tell Principal St. Clair I'm coming to Oak Hills Prep, or I'll be going to Jefferson. Your choice."

I stare my parents down, grateful for the crutches that hide the trembling in my knees and the butterflies in my stomach. My dad is staring at the handful of papers in his hand, the *Jefferson High School* letterhead at the top just visible from under his thumb. "You…"

"Called the school district and talked my way into being enrolled at the public high school across town? Yes, I did." I leave out the part where I pretended to be my mom to do it. I don't want to go to Jefferson, but if it means I can stay in Oak Hills, I'll do whatever I need. Romeo and I will be okay, even if I don't get to go to the same school as him.

I hope so anyway. Hope is all I have left now.

Mom silently takes the papers from Dad's limp fingers. "Juliet." She clears her throat. "Why? Is it about that boy?"

If I could stomp a foot I would. "No, Mom. This is me asking you both to listen to what I want. I don't want to go back to Turkey with you. I don't want to spend my senior year locked up in a tower like Rapunzel. I want one year to be a normal kid. To go to regular classes, to have homework, take pop quizzes, and midterms. I want to go to a school dance, not the embassy balls. I want to stay out too late with my friends and eat Taco Bell at one in the morning on a Saturday night and then have a stomach ache the next day."

Dad's eyebrow pops up at the mention of one a.m. Maybe I shouldn't have said it like that, but I don't care. It's time that they listened to me for once.

I soften my voice, trying to remember the second part of the speech I'd planned for them. "You've had me all to yourselves my whole life and I've never complained. I love that I got to see so many cool parts of the world. But you never let me make any mistakes either. I don't know how I can trust myself to go off to college and be an adult if you never let me have a chance to practice."

"I think you've done plenty of practicing this summer." If it had been a year ago, maybe even three months ago, the tone of my mom's voice would have had me cowering and apologizing.

I sigh, the weight of this conversation settling on my shoulders. "We wouldn't have run away like that if you and the Montgomery's were being reasonable." My words hang in the air between us. The accusation has been haunting us all for weeks now, since the night of the accident, but no one has dared to say it out loud. "Romeo isn't a bad guy—"

"I beg to differ." My dad's interruption has heat flaring in my cheeks.

"Dad." I take a breath before I explode. "You've only had one conversation with him, and it wasn't a conversation. It was you and Uncle Chuck tearing him apart and calling him horrible names. You don't know what he's really like."

"Juliet, please." Mom cuts us both off before an explosion occurs. "You're swaying on your foot, sit down before you hurt yourself."

I sit only so they don't have any extra ammunition against me. "Can we discuss this? Surely…" Dad cuts her off, glaring at me.

"Melinda, what is there to discuss? She wants to stay here where she can continue to see this hoodlum and throw away all of the advantages we've worked so hard to give her." A vein twitches on Dad's forehead. "She's an ungrateful child who's throwing a tantrum because she isn't getting her way."

He doesn't even look at me, talking to Mom as if I'm not even in the room. After experiencing what it's like to have someone talk *to* me, not *at* me, instead of bruising my heart, Dad's words slice through me. Angry tears form in my eyes but I refuse to cry again. They aren't worth my tears. Not anymore.

"I'm. Right. Here." I grind out between my teeth. "I'm not ungrateful. I'm not having a tantrum. I'm telling you—asking you—to listen to me. If I can't stay here with your blessing, I'll stay here without it. I love you both, but I'm not a doll for you to dress up and put on display. I want to live *my* life, not yours."

We sit in silence, my parents staring at me as if for the first time. Maybe it is. Maybe this is the first time they've ever really looked at me and seen me for who I am, not who they assume me to be. I can't blame them. I've spent my whole life fading into the background, living in their shadow, never asking to be seen. I'm as much a stranger to myself as I am to them. But I can't seem to squeeze myself into that shadow, I don't fit anymore.

Finally, I pull my crutches in front of me and push to my foot. "Let me know when you decide which it's going to be. I'm going out with Rosie."

My crutches clack against the hardwood floor as I make my way out the door. My parent's silence is deafening. I didn't want it to be this way.

"Juliet—" I pause in the doorway at the crack in Mom's voice.

"Yeah?" I don't turn to look.

"Be safe."

"I will."

THE SUN warms my skin, an afternoon breeze picking up my hair and tickling my cheek. Eyes closed, I let the heat of it soak into my soul, into the ice cold fear that's been lodged in my gut ever since I watched the ambulance drive away with Romeo.

It's been a week and I haven't heard anything except his seventy-two hour hold was extended to ten days. The girl's chatter washes over me, the fact that the topic of conversation has nothing to do with me or my problems is a relief.

"I don't understand why you don't just say yes. He's asked you out how many times?" There's a pause, then Rosie speaks again. "Why does Tia have any say in it?"

I crack one eye to peek at Nikki, but close it again against the bright light when she speaks. "Because she's the captain."

Rosie scoffs. "Being captain of the dance team doesn't give her the right to decide who you can and can't date, Nikki. That's ridiculous. You need to stand up for yourself. Don't let Tia walk all over you. Do you really think Benny is going to wait around forever?"

There's a rustling noise and someone lays down beside me on the blanket. After I left my parents in the den, Rosie and I picked up Nikki and Melody before swinging through a coffee drive-thru. We're currently camped out on one end of Oak Hills Prep's football field, a picnic of coffee and pastries spread out between us.

"Be nice Rosie. Juliet is the only one of us who's been brave enough to fight for the person she wants to be with." Melody's voice is quiet, sad.

Rosie's response is even softer. "Yeah, well. Our situation is different."

All three girls are quiet long enough that I open my eyes to make sure they haven't left. Rosie and Melody sit shoulder to shoulder on one side of me, Rosie's head resting on Melody's shoulder, both of them staring across the field. As I watch, Melody runs a hand down Rosie's spine, her fingers dancing over the bright blue tank Rosie's wearing. A shiver runs up Rosie's back and a quiet sigh escapes her.

I turn my head away, not wanting to intrude on their moment. Nikki's swiping slowly through pictures on her phone, a sad smile on her face. She has to know Benny feels the same way she does. I've spent enough time with those three boys to know that Benny is as in love with her as she is with him.

"I wish I could make my parents understand that this is what I want, just as much as I want to be with Romeo." I speak the truth without bothering to filter it. If anyone will understand, these girls will. They don't say anything so I keep speaking. "Obviously, I love him and I want to be with him. I'll be devastated if we can't be together. But I still want to stay. Whether or not we're together. For me. I want to stay for me."

I don't dive any deeper into my mixed up feelings about Romeo, not wanting to burden them with my confusion. The only things I'm sure of right now are that I love him and I want to stay in Oak Hills, not run away.

Nikki puts her phone down and lays down next to me, the braids coiled on top of her head so tall they rest in the grass beyond the edge of the blanket. "Do you think your ultimatum will work?"

Rosie laughs, turning to look at us behind Melody's back. "I'm sure it will. No way will they let their precious Juliet go to *Jefferson*. The horror!"

"Whose idea was it to pick that school?" Melody asks. "It's brilliant."

"Mine." I grin. "I looked up which high school in the district had the lowest test scores and graduation rates."

"Who knew you were so devious?" Melody offers a hand for a high five and I slap it.

I never knew I wanted friends like this before. Determination to keep this, no matter what my parents say, settles in my gut.

"I didn't." I shrug and grin. "It's kind of fun. Who knows what other things I'll discover about myself when I get to stay?"

CHAPTER THIRTY-EIGHT

Romeo

I STARE AT the locked medicine cabinet in my bathroom, only my antidepressants are out on the counter. Dad actually did it. I didn't think he would. After all this time, *now* he does something?

"I…" Dad stops, rubs the back of his neck and pulls a face. "Your mom…Every day, I'm terrified I'm going to get a phone call from a hospital. Or I'm going to come home and find her…" He stops, closing his eyes. "She's functional. I know she needs help, but she doesn't want it. I never thought…I never thought that the call I feared the most would be about *you*. I couldn't bear…" His words are halting, unsure. My dad is never unsure.

Before I can shrink into myself, I'm pulled into a bear hug. "I don't want to lose you too, son."

I push against him. "You don't even know me." One of the things the therapist at the rehabilitation center and I talked about was how it felt like my dad abandoned me years ago. That when my mom checked out, he'd been so angry at her for leaving us, but not leaving us, that he'd turned his back on me. And I'd been too afraid of needing him to ask for help.

At least, that's what she says. I'm not sure if that's really true or if I just don't like my dad for being a pompous asshole who expects me to take care of myself at all times. Maybe there's more to Dad's issues than I realized. But either way, the hug is weird.

He lets go but doesn't walk away like I expect. "Sorry. I'll give you space. But the thought of losing you scared the crap out of me. I've had too much time to think about all the things I've missed with you while you were in the hospital. I thought the car accident was bad enough…but it was easy to just be mad at you about that, for making the choice to put yourself and Juliet in danger." He looks past me to my bedroom, to the spot on the carpet where Rosie apparently found me. "But to know that you couldn't see a way out of the situation that I'd put you in. Me and the Caplans." He shakes his head.

I guess my dad's had as much time to think as I have. It's weird.

"Is this your way of saying you won't try to stop Juliet and I from being together? Friends, or whatever it is we are right now?"

He chuckles and rubs my head. Okay, that's also weird, but I don't hate it. A little glow sits in my gut, feeding on the comfort it gives me. "No, I won't stop whatever it is you have with her. She saved your life—how can I be anything but grateful to her?"

A knock on the front door interrupts our strange father-son moment. "I'll get it." Sprinting down the stairs, careful not to bang my arm on the banister, I slide to stop in front of the heavy wood door.

I fling it open, my heart racing. "I—" There's no time to say anything else before a bundle of blonde sunshine is in my arms. Juliet squeezes me as tight as I'm squeezing her. She's mumbling something against my chest but I can't make out the words. Her body pressed against mine, her arms wrapped around my chest, the way the top of her head fits under my chin and her face is buried in the space above my heart is beyond words. It's perfection.

Everything good in the world is wrapped up in my arms. How could anyone expect me to let this go?

My good hand buries itself in her hair as I press kisses to the top of her head. She leans into me, like she would crawl inside my skin if I let her. She's already deep in my soul. The weight of her knocks us both off balance and I fall against the doorframe, keeping her safe from the impact by turning my back to catch us at the last second.

"They're letting me stay." The grin that accompanies her words takes my breath away and it takes another second for her words to filter into my brain.

"You're staying? For real? They're not taking you away?" I run my fingers over her face, her cheeks, her hair. Is this real?

"It was let me stay and go to Oak Hills, or drag me onto the plane trussed like a Thanksgiving turkey. I even threatened to enroll at Jefferson if they wouldn't talk to Principal St. Clair about getting my spot back."

I laugh, the sound unfamiliar after the last few weeks of being stuck with only my own sad thoughts for company. After a pause she laughs with me, her laughter turning to tears before she buries her face in my chest again. I hold her tight while she cries against me.

"I was afraid I would never hear that sound again." Her whisper scrapes at my still tender heart. "I still love you. You know that, right?"

My heart stops, and then it does the strangest thing. It doesn't explode. It doesn't race. My bruised and battered heart takes a deep breath and settles down. It curls up in Juliet's declaration like a warm blanket. Peace. That's what that feeling is. I think.

"I love you too."

This kiss isn't desperate. It's not a battle or a fight or any other feeling doomed to tragedy. It's coming home. It's settling in for the long haul. This kiss is like taking a breath of fresh air after being inside for too long.

My dad clearing his throat behind me startles us apart. "You must be Juliet. It's nice to meet you."

Pulling free of my arms, Juliet peers into my house. As she leans away from me, I help her balance on one leg, picking up the crutches lying haphazardly on the front steps.

"Hi." Her voice is soft, but steady. Looking up and tucking one crutch under my arm, I'm in time to see Dad reaching out a hand to her. "It's nice to meet you."

"Likewise. I owe you a huge thanks, young lady." Dad's voice cracks a little and he pauses. "I'm so glad my son has someone like you on his side. I want you to know, you'll always be welcome here in our home."

Who is this guy and what did he do with my grumpy father? Juliet tips her head in acknowledgement and gives him a fake smile. "I agree. I'm glad Romeo has someone on his side, too."

Awkward silence fills the house. I'm fighting back a laugh at how neatly Juliet put Dad in his place—she's such a diplomat, even if she won't admit it. Dad is bobbing his head like he's about to speak but hasn't figured out the words.

"Right…" He finally forms words. "Well. I'll be in my office if you need anything." He jerks a thumb towards his office door and disappears a moment later.

The laughter I've been holding in bursts out of me. I wish I could sweep Juliet up in my arms and spin her around, but between the casts on my arm and her leg it doesn't seem smart. "Oh my God, Angel. I've never seen anyone put him in his place like that."

She beams at me, the warmth of her real smile worming it's way inside me, soothing the jagged edges that always pop up when I talk to my dad. "I'll have to tell Kim it worked."

"Who's Kim?"

"My therapist." Juliet doesn't give me a chance to respond before she's tugging me towards the front door. "Come on. I wasn't sure what kind of reception I'd get so Rosie and Marcus helped me plan a surprise."

She swings away on her crutches, out the front door and down the steps, leaving me to catch up.

I can't hold her hand while she's on the crutches so I stroke the back of her neck instead. "Your parents took you to a therapist?" Surely her parents would object, they don't seem like the kind of people who've moved into the twenty-first century with the rest of us.

"Hold on, I'll tell you everything later. First you have to appreciate my masterpiece."

I look past her to see a matching set of Adirondack chairs set up in the grass that bridges our two front lawns, a small table between them. "What's this?"

"I wasn't sure if you would be allowed on Caplan property so I set it up so that *technically* you could stay on your side and I could stay on mine." She grins at me, obviously proud of herself. "Wanna have a picnic with me?"

This time I do attempt to pick her up, my good arm wrapping around her waist, my broken arm braced on the outside. I swing us both in a circle, peppering kisses on her beautiful face while she laughs.

"You are utterly brilliant." Purposefully setting her down in the chair on the Montgomery side of the property line, I can't resist dropping another kiss on her lips before settling myself in the chair on the Caplan side. Chuck and Cathy better get used to having me around.

She's arranged a spread of cheese, crackers, fruit, and cookies on the table, but the thing I'm starving for is her. I'll eat the food anyway, because it's food and I'm a growing boy.

"So, tell me about Kim." I twist in my chair so I can see her while I pick up a cracker and crunch down on it.

Juliet sighs and leans back against the chair, the sunlight catching her pale hair and skin.

"Well, Rosie and I had a lot of time on our hands while we were locked in the tower." She points up at her bedroom window. "We'd been watching TV and saw a commercial for those online therapists and figured it was worth a shot. I'd brought it up to my parents earlier, but Mom only suggested I talk to a pastor." She shudders and I can't blame her.

"So you and Rosie set it up? But we're minors, didn't they need your parent's permission?" I stuff another cracker topped with a slice of cheese in my mouth.

Juliet shakes her head. "Apparently not. I think once you're over the age of fourteen or something, they're not required to notify your parents."

She picks up a little cluster of grapes and leans back against the chair. "You said it yourself, they gave me that credit card to use while I was here." Turning her head, she grins at me. "So what if I used it to pay for real therapy instead of retail therapy?"

We share a laugh and dig into the picnic she arranged, feeding each other and giggling over how dumb we must look to the neighbors.

I pause, a grape pinched between my fingers. "I can't believe you get to stay. That we're going to get to be together. It doesn't seem real."

"It's real. It better be after how hard I fought my parents to let me stay." There's a sadness to her voice but I don't comment on it, not wanting to make her feel worse. "But, um, we need to talk about some things."

A brick settles in my belly and for a second I regret all the cheese I just ate. "Yeah. I figured."

Juliet's gray-blue eyes meet mine and they're filled with determination and hope, easing the worry creeping into my heart. "Hey, nothing bad. We just need to, you know…maybe not almost die again, okay?"

"And here I thought you were going to say we needed to decide what to wear for the first day of school."

Juliet bounces a grape off my jaw. "I'm serious, Romeo. I'm staying for senior year no matter what happens between us. But I can't be the only thing tethering you to the ground. I need to know you're sticking it out because you want to, not just because of me."

Even though her words slice into me, I still want to reach out and pull her into my arms, wipe away the tear that's rolling down her cheek. She's not sure she wants to be with me? Is it because I'm just too much?

"What happens if we aren't together? I have to be honest—I don't know if I can bear the idea of you being with anyone else." Before I can promise her anything, I have to know the answer. I'm tempted to lie and tell her exactly what she wants to hear, not give her a reason to back away from being with me. I need her. "I've done a lot of work on myself in the last couple of weeks, but I know I'm not ready for that."

I don't want her to be with me out of guilt. But I can't lie and say I don't need her.

Her eyebrows shoot up and a tiny gasp escapes her. "That wasn't what I meant! I just...maybe I said it wrong." She tugs on the ends of her hair, her bottom lip caught between her teeth.

I lean back in my chair, eyes closed and heart racing, waiting for her to explain.

"Romeo?"

I crack an eye and look at her, dreading what I might see. She's turned awkwardly in her chair to face me, arms hooked over the edge and a fierce look in those pale eyes.

"Romeo Montgomery, you listen to me and quit jumping to conclusions."

I fully open my eyes at her tone and push to sit up a little straighter.

"I love you. I *want* to be with you. If I didn't, why would I have fought so hard to be allowed to stay? *You* gave me a reason to push back, to stand up to my parents and stop letting them dictate everything I do. Before I met you, I didn't have a reason to fight for myself. Now I do."

She takes a deep breath, her shoulders and face softening. "I know you love me. I know it like I know the grass is green. But life is messy and unpredictable and it doesn't always work out like in my books with a happily ever after. The car accident? Either one of us could have died. There's no way anyone could have predicted it."

"What I'm saying is, I love you so much that all I want is for you to have the very best life you could possibly imagine. I *want* to be in it. But if, for some reason, I can't be—I want you to have it anyway. I can't be the only thing that keeps you wanting to know what happens tomorrow."

Her words seep into my heart, taking root. The peace that I felt when she launched into my arms earlier comes back, pushing away the panic. If it wasn't so hard for either of us to navigate our broken body parts I would hold her. Instead I reach across and grab her hand, squeezing her fingers.

"I promise to try. Every day."

She squeezes back, ducking down to press a kiss to my knuckles. "That's all I need."

Juliet

STARING AT the entrance to Oak Hills Prep, a sense of déjà vu washes over me. How many times have I imagined myself walking into school on the first day of senior year, a pack of friends waiting for me? And a cute boyfriend carrying my backpack for me?

Of course, I never imagined he'd be carrying my backpack because I'd be on crutches. And I didn't think the friends would be there to help me find my locker and classes because I was brand new to the school.

But I don't mind, I'm ready for a new adventure.

"Earth to Juliet!" Rosie calls from the open doorway. "Are you coming?"

Romeo's hand drops onto my shoulder. Looking up at him, at the determination in his eyes, warmth settles in my belly. "I don't know why I'm so nervous." I whisper just to him.

Leaning down, he presses a kiss to the side of my head. "You got this, Angel. I have faith in you."

I have faith in you.

It's become our mantra, our secret code when either of us feels wobbly inside. A little reminder that we've already gone through hell and now we're on the other side. That now is the time to build new foundations, to sweep away the old fear and step into the unknown together.

He'd whispered it in my ear last night while I was sobbing in his arms. Saying goodbye to my parents had been harder than I'd ever imagined. My dad hasn't spoken to me since I threw down my ultimatum. Even as he agreed to it and contacted Principal St. Clair, it was done silently, resentfully.

"I have faith in you, too. We got this, right?" I push up on my crutches to return the kiss and let Romeo lead me through the front doors. Lockers line the walls, broken up by doors leading to various classrooms. It's all so perfectly ordinary.

I love it.

Mom won't talk to me about anything other than the logistics of my new life here. She and Cathy set me up with my own bank account that will have money deposited into it regularly, on the condition that I keep my grades up and stay out of trouble. It's a small price to pay for the freedom of being here.

I'm sure they wanted to make staying away from Romeo a condition of me staying here but weren't willing to risk the gossip that would result from me following through on my threat to go to Jefferson.

Kim, my therapist, is helping me stay firm in my boundaries. Even when the silent treatment gets to me and I want to crumble into a pile of people-pleasing mush. I hate that they can't see how much I still love them. I'm still their good girl—I just don't want to be their doormat. Maybe one day they'll come around.

Nikki, Rosie, and Melody crowd around me while Romeo greets Benny and Marcus. "You ready for this?" Rosie grins at me while she takes my backpack from Romeo. "The boys have to get to practice soon, so say goodbye to lover-boy and follow me."

The girls offered to meet me here unreasonably early, so they can show me where my classes are. They're really good friends.

Despite his broken arm, Romeo hasn't lost his place on the varsity baseball team since the season won't start for a couple of months. But they still have some kind of weightlifting routine they do in the off-season and he's working on healing his arm and getting it back in shape. I know nothing about baseball, but I'm glad he's planning for something in the spring.

Every time he talks about something happening in the future I breathe a little easier.

An arm slides around my waist and pulls me to the side. Marcus sweeps my crutches out from under my arms as I fall against Romeo and the lockers. "Well, that wasn't quite as smooth as I thought it was going to be." His eyes are bright and laughing, a hint of mischief sparkling at me. "I was aiming to sweep you off your feet, not smash you into the walls, sorry."

Giggling, I lean against him, letting him take my weight. "It would have been very romantic if it had worked." I won't tell him that the theatrics are a relief, proof that he's feeling more like himself. "I'll see you in third period, right?"

Romeo's grimace is comical, that animated face telling everyone exactly what he thinks of the class. "Yup. Can't wait."

I smack his arm. "It's just econ, how bad can it be?"

The words are hardly out of my mouth before everyone is talking over each other, to explain to me just how awful Mr. Hardacre is. I let them talk, nodding, but secretly I'm so excited to have teachers other than my mom, I don't care how tough the teachers are. This year is going to be amazing.

"Rome, we gotta go," Benny finally says, cutting everyone's tirades off.

"I'll catch up in a second." Romeo waves them off, his heartbeat beneath my hand on his chest speeding up. "Go away, Rosie."

"You have thirty seconds, then we're stealing her." Nikki answers instead of Rosie, tugging her down the hall after Marcus and Benny. "We didn't get here this early to watch your PDA."

The second they leave, Romeo is kissing me, his hands on my back pulling me close. I can taste the hot chocolate we had for breakfast on his lips, and feel his breathing picking up speed.

"Are you going to be okay?" I whisper against his lips, my fingers caressing his cheek.

He pulls back, resting his forehead against mine. "Shakespeare cheated I think."

"What do you mean?" His breath is warm and real against my lips. I don't let him answer, capturing his lips with mine instead. If I could pour my own strength into him I would. But I'll do the next best thing—I'll love him fiercely and protect his fragile heart with every beat of my own.

"Having everyone die at the end is the easy way out. Living happily ever after is so much harder."

"Is that what we're doing?" My words are laced with amusement and he grins down at me. My Romeo, my trouble-maker. Alive. Healing.

"Hopefully."

The End

If you or someone you know needs help, call the National Suicide Prevention Hotline at 800-273-8255

If you're in the UK call Samaritans at 116 123

Most importantly, talk to someone. A friend, a pet, a loved one, a stranger. There is someone out there who wants you to be there tomorrow. Reach out and someone will reach back.

ACKNOWLEDGEMENTS

Readers, this book was hard to write. It was so hard I almost gave up halfway through. And not just because it's so much darker than my previous books, although there was that too.

I can say it's because my marriage fell apart right before I started working on it. I can blame it on my laptop dying halfway through the process. I could even say it was because I had people in and out of my home over the summer and my schedule got thrown out the window. Those reasons are all true.

But the real truth is that I was scared of this book. I dove into it willfully oblivious to how hard the end was going to be to write. How close to home those feelings would hit and how terrified I would feel about trying to do them justice. And as hard and as dark as this book is (I avoided writing chapter thirty-four for as long as I possibly could—my house was *very* clean for a couple of weeks), in the end I knew I couldn't skip the hard parts and still do these characters and their story justice.

I've always been annoyed by the original story of Romeo and Juliet. Annoyed at it being held up as the pinnacle of romance, when in reality the Romeo that Shakespeare wrote charges through the play like a bowling ball, knocking down everyone around him while spouting ridiculous poetic phrases. Juliet of the play makes only one decision of her own and it ultimately kills her. It's all so needlessly tragic and frustrating. And poor Rosaline never even gets to appear on stage!

So I set out to tell my own version. I hope you enjoyed it, I hope it made you feel something. I loved every painful minute that went into writing it. The following people are the real reason I made it to the end of this book.

Lis—how can I thank you for all the small ways you support me? You're my favorite human I didn't give birth to, and always will be. River walks and sitting in the grass together this summer kept me sane.

Las—my friend, my mentor, my confidant. We will get those matching tattoos one day, I promise.

Danielle—Romeo is more than just a love-struck show-off because of you. You helped me make him real.

Spark Notes and BIC highlighters—you know what you did.

Prokofiev and YouTube—Thank you for writing such gorgeous music and for letting me keep the Royal Ballet's film of the ballet on loop.

And to my readers who stuck with me as this book was delayed and delayed and delayed. Thank you. I hope it was worth it.

ON POINTE (COMPLETE SERIES)

Hannah has to decide which dream is worth
fighting for—ballet or the boy?

Toe to Toe
Head to Head
Face to Face
Heart to Heart

OAK HILLS

Welcome to Oak Hills where you'll find heart-shattering love
and tragedy, and things are always darkest just before dawn.

Crossed Stars
Third Wheel (coming 2022)

ABOUT THE AUTHOR

Penelope Freed lives in the Pacific Northwest where you can find her learning how to drive in the rain, walking her dog and making a mess in the kitchen. Her daughter thinks she's a little bit bonkers and really hates it when she dances embarrassingly in public. Which she does, often.

After a lifetime in the ballet world, Penelope decided to start writing down the stories in her head instead of narrating her ballet classes with them—her former students are very thankful for this decision. Now, Penelope writes stories about dreamers, just like she is, who are willing to do whatever it takes to make those dreams come true.

Keep up with Penelope by subscribing to her newsletter here: sendfox.com/penelopefreedbooks

INSTAGRAM: penelopefreedbooks
TIKTOK: penelopefreed

9 781736 489345